# NAMELESS

# NAMELESS

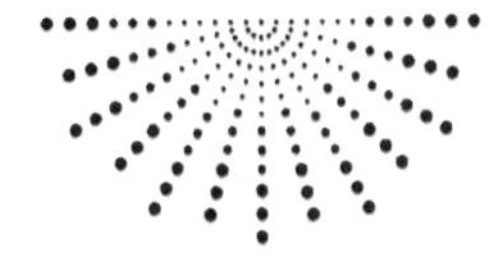

JEFFREY TRAVERS

# CONTENTS

# PROLOGUE

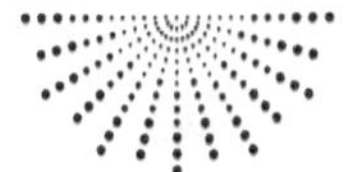

A dimly lit night stretched over the Roman colony, an outpost standing far beyond the empire's borders. The usual stillness of the evening had been shattered. Terror streaked through the darkness, carried on the streaming voices of men, women, and children. Horses reared and screamed, their panicked cries blending with the frantic bleating of livestock. The very air trembled under the weight of fear.

Nature itself had fallen silent. The creaking of crickets had ceased. The croaking of toads was no more. Even the wind seemed to recoil, unwilling to carry the sounds of the horror that unfolded. Only the guttural, wet symphony of death remained —gasps, gurgles, the sickening crunch of bone beneath monstrous strength.

No one was spared. The streets ran red as soldiers barked orders, their voices cracking with terror. Swords flashed in the firelight, but their strikes met nothing but air or flesh too dense to cut. They fought without knowing their enemy, their formations breaking like sand against a tide. None were safe in this dark awakening.

Death had come to this colony. And death would collect in blood.

Then, from the shadows, they emerged.

The monsters were as black as the abyss, towering like ancient oaks. Their eyes burned crimson, molten pools of hatred and hunger. Their claws, jagged and wickedly sharp, were the last thing many would ever see before their bodies were torn asunder. Devilish growls rumbled from their gaping jaws, vibrating through the earth itself.

They were not men. They were not beasts. They were death given form.

And they would leave nothing behind.

# RISE OF ROME AND THE CALL TO MAXIMUS

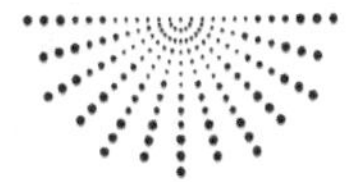

*The Bustling City of Rome*

Rome was a city unlike any other in the known world. Its grandeur stretched beyond the imaginations of travelers who flocked to its gates, and its streets were alive with the pulse of the empire's heart. Towering aqueducts carried water across hills and valleys, a feat of engineering that proclaimed the ingenuity of its people. The Colosseum loomed on the horizon, its arches standing as a testament to the might of Rome's gladiators and the indomitable spirit of its citizens.

The Forum was a hub of activity, with merchants shouting their wares—fine silks from the East, rare spices from the Indies, and glimmering trinkets forged from the empire's vast reserves of gold. Senators in flowing togas strode through the avenues; their conversations tinged with ambition and intrigue. Children darted between carts and horses, their laughter a melody that softened the hard edges of the city's commerce.

Above the bustling streets, the imperial palace stood on Palatine Hill, its golden domes and marble colonnades reflecting the afternoon sun. The palace was a beacon of Rome's unchallenged supremacy, a reminder to all who gazed upon it of the power wielded within its walls.

Yet beneath the surface of the city's vibrancy lay whispers of unease. Rumors of a growing threat in the North spread like wildfire among the citizens. The empire was vast, its borders difficult to defend, and the thought of an enemy slipping past the legions chilled even the most confident Romans. The arrival of a bloodied survivor at the city gates only fueled these fears.

*The Survivor's Arrival*

The sun dipped low on the horizon, casting long shadows across the towering gates of Rome. The sentries stationed atop the walls were accustomed to the comings and goings of merchants, soldiers, and citizens, but the sight of a lone rider stumbling toward the gate on a weary horse brought them to full attention.

"Open the gates!" one of the guards called, his voice urgent.

The gates creaked open, and the rider collapsed from his saddle as he passed through. His armor was in tatters, blood and grime caking every inch of his body. His eyes, wide with terror, darted between the faces of those who rushed to his aid.

"Centurion Brutus!" a guard exclaimed, recognizing the soldier. "What has happened? Where is your unit?"

Brutus's voice was hoarse, his words broken by gasps for air. "Gone... all gone. They came in the night... monsters, beasts from the depths of hell. We stood no chance."

The guards exchanged uneasy glances as Brutus continued, his hands trembling. "They were massive, their skin harder than any armor, their claws ripping through men as if they were parchment. They drank our blood and fed on our flesh... the screams..."

"Take him to the palace," the guard captain ordered. "The emperor must hear of this."

Brutus was lifted onto a cart and escorted through the city, his presence drawing the attention of citizens who whispered and pointed as he passed. By the time he reached the imperial palace, word of his arrival had spread, and the council was already assembled in anticipation.

*The Emperor's Palace: A Gathering of Power*

The grand hall of the imperial palace was alive with tension. The senators sat in a semicircle, their flowing togas marking their status, but their words betrayed their unease. Emperor Gaius Julius Augustus sat at the head of the assembly, his expression grave as he listened to Centurion Brutus recount the horrors of the northern frontier. His voice faltered, his gaze distant as he relived the nightmare.

"Three garrisons wiped out in a single night," Brutus concluded, his hands trembling. "We tried... but they were too many. Too strong."

"Monsters!" Portius Aralus scoffed, his tone dismissive. "This is nothing more than the ravings of a soldier broken by fear. Perhaps this garrison fell to barbarian hordes, and he seeks to save face with tales of demons."

Claudius Di Vinci stood abruptly; his golden brooch catching the torchlight. "And what if he speaks the truth? What if this threat is unlike anything we have faced? Shall we dismiss it and risk the empire's ruin?"

Portius sneered. "Then we should call upon one of Rome's steadier hands. General Severus commands the Sixth Legion. He is disciplined, loyal, and not prone to... unpredictable actions."

"Disciplined, yes," Di Vinci replied sharply. "But Severus has not won a significant campaign in years. This threat requires not just discipline but brilliance. Someone who can think like a soldier and a predator."

The emperor leaned forward, his voice calm but authoritative, "And you propose Maximus?"

"Of course," Di Vinci said, his tone unwavering. "He is the only one who has faced the impossible and triumphed."

The chamber erupted into murmurs, many senators expressing their discomfort.

"Maximus?" Senator Gallus exclaimed, his voice trembling. "That man has no love for Rome's politics. He spurns our invitations to the Senate and mocks our traditions. He is a sword without a sheath—a weapon that cuts indiscriminately."

"Precisely why he is the best choice," Di Vinci countered. "While you wring your hands, Maximus wins wars. He does not seek our approval, only victory."

The emperor raised his hand, silencing the debate. "Enough. Maximus is not bound to this city, nor should he be. He fights for Rome, not for politics. He will be summoned."

The senators fell silent, though their unease lingered. Augustus turned to his steward. "Prepare the summons. Send my personal seal. And send riders who will not fail."

Portius Aralus was a man born into privilege, yet he had always felt overshadowed by the great men of Rome. From a young age, his father, a prominent senator, often reminded him that power was fleeting unless wielded with precision. "The true rulers of Rome," his father would say, "are not the ones who wear the laurel crown, but the ones who place it upon their heads." These words shaped Portius's worldview, instilling in him a hunger for influence that went beyond wealth or titles.

While others sought glory on the battlefield, Portius honed his skills in the Senate. He became a master of rhetoric, charming allies and undermining rivals with calculated subtlety. Yet, his ambitions did not stop at the Senate. He had his eyes on the ultimate prize—the imperial throne itself.

Portius's wife, Livia, was the keystone to his plans. Their marriage was not one of love but of strategy. Livia was the sister of General Severus, commander of the Sixth Legion, a man known for his discipline and loyalty to tradition. Severus was everything Portius was not—a soldier beloved by his men with a reputation for fairness and honor. But Severus lacked the political acumen to navigate Rome's treacherous waters. Portius saw this as an opportunity.

Over years of carefully cultivated dinners and whispered conversations, Portius positioned himself as Severus's staunchest advocate in the Senate. He painted the general as a man of integrity and stability, contrasting him with the more controversial figures like Maximus. Severus, in turn, began to view Portius as a trusted advisor, unaware of the deeper ambitions driving his brother-in-law's loyalty.

When Emperor Augustus proposed summoning Maximus to lead the campaign against the northern threat, Portius saw an opportunity to weaken the emperor's judgment and advance his own agenda. He quickly rallied a group of like-minded senators—men who resented Maximus's disdain for politics and feared his growing reputation among the people.

That evening, Portius convened a secret meeting in the atrium of his villa. The attendees included Senators Gallus, Calpurnius, and Drusus—each with their own grudges or ambitions. Over goblets of imported wine, Portius laid out his case.

"Maximus is a sword without a sheath," Portius began, his tone calm but resolute. "He is a man of war, not of Rome. His victories may inspire the legions, but his disdain for the Senate is dangerous. Do we really want a man like that to command this campaign? To be celebrated as a hero of Rome?"

Gallus frowned. "The people love him. If he succeeds, his influence will only grow. It could threaten the balance of power."

"Exactly," Portius said, seizing the moment. "And then there is the question of loyalty. Maximus fights for glory, not for Rome. General Severus, on the other hand, is a man of discipline, a man who respects tradition and authority. He has served this Senate faithfully for decades."

Drusus leaned forward. "But Severus has not won a major campaign in years. How do we convince the emperor to place him in command instead of Maximus?"

Portius smiled, the expression more calculating than warm. "We don't need to convince Augustus directly. We plant seeds of doubt. Whisper to him that Maximus is too impulsive, too reckless for this mission. Remind him that Severus is a safe choice—a loyal servant of Rome who will follow orders without question."

"And if the emperor doesn't listen?" Calpurnius asked.

Portius's gaze hardened. "Then we make it impossible for Maximus to succeed. If he falters, even for a moment, we will call for his replacement. The people may love him, but they will not forgive failure."

The senators exchanged uneasy glances but ultimately nodded in agreement.

Portius's plot extended beyond the immediate goal of undermining Maximus. He knew that discrediting the general would also weaken Emperor Augustus, whose decision to summon Maximus could be painted as a lapse in judgment. If Severus succeeded in the northern campaign, it would not only bolster his reputation but also solidify Portius's influence in both the Senate and the legions.

After the senators had left, In private, Portius confided in Livia, knowing she could sway her brother if necessary. "You must remind Severus of his duty to Rome—and to us," he told her. "His victories will not just secure the empire's borders but also pave the way for a brighter future. For our family."

Livia, though skeptical of her husband's ambitions, knew better than to oppose him. She relayed Portius's words to Severus, emphasizing the importance of the campaign not just for Rome but for their family's legacy.

The next day, leading up to the arrival of Maximus, Portius maneuvered carefully. He met privately with Augustus, framing his concerns as those of a loyal servant.

"Maximus is a brilliant tactician," Portius admitted, his tone measured. "But brilliance is often accompanied by recklessness. Rome cannot afford recklessness now. General Severus may lack Maximus's flair, but he is steady, dependable. He will not gamble with the lives of our soldiers."

Augustus listened but remained noncommittal. Portius could see the doubt in his eyes, and it gave him hope.

The night was heavy with whispers of power and intrigue as Senator Claudius Di Vinci entered the private chambers of Emperor Augustus. The room was lit by a golden glow from oil lamps, casting long shadows on the intricate frescoes that adorned the walls. Augustus, seated on a high-backed chair, looked up as Di Vinci approached. His expression was calm, but his eyes betrayed the weariness of a man burdened with the weight of empire.

"Claudius," Augustus said warmly, gesturing for him to sit. "To what do I owe the pleasure of your visit at this late hour?"

Di Vinci sat but did not relax. His demeanor was grave, his usual wit replaced by solemn determination. "I come to speak of Maximus and the campaign against the northern threat," he began. "But more importantly, I come to speak of Portius."

Augustus's expression hardened. "Portius was here not long ago. He made a case for General Severus to lead the campaign, citing Maximus's recklessness. I listened, but I have known Portius long enough to see the shadows behind his words."

Di Vinci nodded. "Portius plays a long game, Caesar. His loyalty lies not with Rome but with his own ambitions. Supporting Severus, his brother-in-law, is merely the first move in his quest for the throne. If Severus gains glory from this campaign, Portius's influence will grow unchecked."

Augustus leaned forward, his brow furrowing. "And what would you have me do, Claudius? Severus is a loyal servant of Rome, and Portius, for all his flaws, remains a skilled senator. Discrediting them outright could create more enemies than allies."

Di Vinci's voice grew firmer. "Then let Maximus prove

his worth. Let him lead this campaign and silence Portius with victory. But more than that, let me accompany him."

The emperor blinked, taken aback. "You? On a battlefield? Claudius, you are a senator, not a soldier. Your place is here, guiding Rome through diplomacy, not spilling blood on foreign soil."

Di Vinci's expression softened, but his resolve did not waver. "Caesar, my place is wherever Rome needs me most. This is not just about the campaign; it is about the legacy of our empire. Portius's schemes threaten the balance we have worked so hard to maintain. If Maximus succeeds, it will strengthen your reign and weaken those who plot against you. And if I am there, I can ensure the Senate's interests are preserved."

Augustus sighed, rubbing his temples. "You understand the dangers of this request? You could lose your life out there. War is not a game, Claudius. It is chaos, and it does not care for names or titles."

Di Vinci smiled faintly, a flicker of his usual humor returning. "And what a glorious death it would be, Caesar. To die not in the comfort of a villa but on the field of battle, fighting for Rome. That is how men are remembered. That is how the name Di Vinci will finally mean something."

Augustus's gaze softened, his respect for his old friend evident. "Your name already means something, Claudius. You have been my confidant, my advisor, and my friend for years. Rome owes you much."

Di Vinci shook his head. "You and I both know, Caesar, that only those who have bled and conquered are spoken of in the corridors of power. The poets do not sing of words and counsel; they sing of swords and triumph."

The emperor studied him for a long moment before nodding slowly. "Very well. But Maximus must approve. He will not welcome you easily, Claudius. You must convince him yourself."

Di Vinci rose, his determination unshaken. "Leave that part to me, Caesar. Maximus and I are not so different, even if he doesn't see it yet."

As he turned to leave, Augustus called out to him. "Claudius," he said, his voice softer now, almost fatherly. "Take care of yourself. Rome cannot afford to lose men like you."

Di Vinci paused at the doorway, a faint smile on his lips. "Rome will not lose me so easily, Caesar. But if it must, let it be in service to her glory."

As he departed, Augustus leaned back in his chair, the weight of the empire pressing heavier on his shoulders. He knew that both Portius and Claudius represented different sides of the Senate—ambition and loyalty, shadow and light. But in the end, it would be men like Maximus who would decide the fate of Rome, with men like Claudius at their side.

*Maximus's Camp: Bonds Forged in Fire*

The camp of General Maximus was a world apart from the politics of Rome. Soldiers drilled in disciplined formations, their movements sharp and precise. Blacksmiths hammered steel, their rhythmic strikes echoing across the rugged landscape. At the heart of the camp stood Maximus's tent, a modest but commanding structure.

Inside, Maximus sat with his seven mighty men, their bond forged in countless battles. Lugo, the giant, leaned casually against a post, his massive axe nearby. Conan, the barbarian, toyed with the hilt of his broad sword. Ronan polished his blade with the precision of a craftsman. Han and Lee, the nimble brothers, exchanged whispers in their native tongue. Sheba inspected her whip-sword with a critical eye while the priest sat apart, lost in quiet contemplation.

"It's been two years," Conan said, breaking the silence. "Two years since we last marched. Do you think the gods grow bored of us?"

Maximus smiled faintly. "The gods don't grow bored, Conan. They wait. And when the time is right, they choose their champions."

"Champions?" Ronan smirked. "Or pawns in a game we'll never understand?"

"Call it what you will," Maximus replied, his tone sharpening. "But if the gods have chosen us, then we must be ready."

Their conversation was interrupted by the sound of galloping hooves. Two riders approached the camp, their horses kicking up clouds of dust. The first, a black stallion, carried Titus, a veteran with weathered features and armor scarred by battle. The second, a gray mare, carried Cletus, younger and less seasoned, his wide eyes betraying his nerves.

The riders slowed as they neared the perimeter, but a wall of armed soldiers blocked their path. The Seventh Legion was fiercely protective of their leader, and they were not about to allow strangers into their camp unchallenged.

"Halt!" barked a centurion, stepping forward. "State your business."

Titus dismounted, holding up the emperor's seal. "We come bearing a message for General Maximus from Emperor Augustus himself."

The soldiers exchanged glances but did not move. "You'll wait until we clear it with the general," the centurion said.

Cletus bristled. "Do you know who we are? We ride under the emperor's orders!"

"And we serve the general," the centurion replied curtly. "Stand down or turn around."

The tension was broken when Ronan appeared, his sword resting lazily on his shoulder. "If they're lying, they'll die. Let them through."

The riders were escorted to Maximus's tent, where the general and his men awaited them. Titus stepped forward and presented the golden medallion, bowing deeply.

"General Maximus," Titus said, his voice steady. "The emperor commands your presence in Rome. A great threat looms over the North, and only you and your men can stop it."

Maximus took the medallion, his expression unreadable. "What kind of threat?"

Titus hesitated. "Three garrisons have fallen. The survivors speak of... monsters. Creatures beyond comprehension."

The men exchanged uneasy glances. Sheba frowned. "Monsters? This sounds like a fairy tale."

"Fairy tale or not, Rome calls," Maximus said, his tone firm. He looked at his men, his voice carrying the weight of a leader. "For two years, we have waited. The gods choose their champions, and now they have chosen us. Prepare the horses. We ride at dawn."

*Fireside Resolve*

That evening, the mighty men gathered around a crackling fire, their camaraderie as strong as their swords. Laughter mingled with the scent of roasted meat as they shared tales of past battles. But beneath the mirth lay an unspoken tension.

"Monsters," Conan said, his voice heavy with skepticism. "What do you think we're really facing?"

Maximus stared into the flames, his expression calm but resolute. "This medallion carries on one side the face of the emperor and on the other side, mine... I promised to answer this call no matter what. And the emperor gave me these titanium swords as a gift." He looked down at his beautiful swords. "It doesn't matter what they are. Rome needs us, and we will answer. The gods have chosen us, and we will not fail."

Lugo raised his mug. "To the gods and to the glory of Rome!"

The others echoed the toast, their voices strong. Beyond the camp's perimeter, the wind carried the faint howl of wolves. Somewhere in the darkness, an enemy awaited. And tomorrow, the Seventh Legion would ride to meet it.

2

# THE EMPEROR'S BANQUET AND THE HIDDEN THREAT

*The Arrival in Rome*

The journey to Rome took two days. The Seventh Legion left behind the rugged plains of the frontier, riding through rolling hills and into the heart of the empire. As they approached the city, the towering walls of Rome came into view, crowned by sentries who stood watch with unyielding vigilance. Beyond the gates, the sounds of the bustling city rose like a chorus—vendors shouting their wares, children laughing, and the rhythmic clatter of cart-wheels on cobblestone streets.

Maximus and his mighty men rode into the city with a thousand soldiers trailing behind. The citizens turned their heads to watch, their murmurs a mixture of awe and unease. The sight of the legendary general and his entourage was rare and always carried the weight of both promise and peril.

At the edge of the city, they were greeted by Senator

Claudius Di Vinci, who arrived in a gilded chariot drawn by white Persian horses. His attendants dismounted first, one stepping forward to address Maximus.

"General Maximus," the squire said with a low bow. "You stand in the presence of Senator Claudius Di Vinci, Rome's wealthiest and most esteemed—"

"I don't know his name," Maximus interrupted, his tone sharp, "and I don't care for wealth. Speak plainly."

Di Vinci himself stepped down from the chariot, his expression a mix of irritation and admiration. "General, it is my honor to welcome you to Rome," he saw Sheba and gave a slight bow, but her expression remained iced. "The emperor awaits your presence at the palace. However, your soldiers must remain outside the walls. The city cannot bear such a large force within."

Maximus dismounted, his towering presence casting a shadow over the senator. "My men stay ready outside the gates. Only my chosen will accompany me."

Di Vinci bowed slightly, though his expression soured. "As you wish, General. My villa has been prepared for your comfort before tonight's banquet."

*The Emperor's Banquet*

The emperor's banquet hall was a spectacle of opulence. Marble columns rose to a domed ceiling painted with scenes of Rome's victories. Gold and silver adorned every table, while the air was filled with the aromas of roasted meats, spiced wine, and freshly baked bread. Musicians played soft melodies as dancers performed for the assembled guests, their movements fluid and hypnotic.

Maximus and his mighty men entered, their presence commanding the attention of the entire hall. Clad in robes provided by Di Vinci's servants, they looked every bit the part of Rome's heroes, though their discomfort with such finery was evident. They were greeted by Emperor Augustus himself, who descended the steps of his throne to meet them.

"General Maximus," Augustus said, his voice carrying across the hall. "You honor us with your presence."

Maximus bowed his head slightly. "I am here because Rome calls, not for the honor."

The emperor's lips curled into a faint smile. "And that is why you are Rome's greatest asset."

As the banquet commenced, Maximus sat at the emperor's table, surrounded by senators and military advisors. His mighty men took seats nearby, their eyes scanning the room, ever watchful.

*The Emperor's Plea*

Later, Augustus led Maximus to a private courtyard, away from the noise and spectacle of the banquet. Lanterns cast a warm glow over the garden, and the faint hum of cicadas filled the air.

"I summoned you because Rome faces a threat unlike any before," Augustus began, his tone grave. "The northern garrisons have fallen. Three entire legions wiped out in a matter of days."

"I've heard the reports," Maximus said. "Your messenger spoke of creatures. Monsters."

"Yes," Augustus confirmed. "The survivors describe beings of immense size and strength. They move with unnatural speed and tear through men as if they were paper. Their skins are said to be harder than steel, and their blood burns like acid."

Maximus's brow furrowed. "And you believe these accounts?"

"I do," Augustus replied. "Brutus, the centurion who survived, saw these creatures with his own eyes. His account was... unshakable."

"What do you need of me, Caesar?"

"I need you to find the source of this threat and eliminate it. If we do not act swiftly, these creatures will reach Rome, and our walls will not hold."

Maximus nodded slowly. "We'll ride at first light."

## *Di Vinci's Proposition*

After the banquet, Di Vinci hosted Maximus and his men at his luxurious villa. The air was filled with the sounds of laughter and music, the tables laden with delicacies from across the empire. Maximus, however, remained aloof, his mind already on the mission ahead.

Di Vinci approached him, holding a goblet of wine. "A man like you must tire of battle," the senator said. "Surely you've dreamed of a life beyond the sword."

Maximus glanced at him. "My life is the sword."

"Perhaps," Di Vinci said, lowering his voice. "But I

could make it more comfortable. Let me fund this campaign. My wealth could ensure you have every resource at your disposal."

"And what do you want in return?"

"A name," Di Vinci admitted. "A name worthy of Rome. Let me ride with you, and together, we'll ensure my legacy."

Maximus considered the proposition, his gaze steady. "This isn't about legacy, Senator. It's about survival. If you want to join, you'll fight as we fight. No special treatment."

Di Vinci hesitated but nodded. "Agreed."

In the open court of Senator Di Vinci's estate, under the Twilight of a crescent moon, Sheba trained with her whiplash and her blade, demonstrating mystery in her craft. A voice broke the harmony of her dance. "You fight like someone with nothing to lose." Di Vinci was standing beside a pillar on his porch.

Sheba (without looking up), "And you talk like someone who doesn't know what a fight is."

Sweat dripping off her brow, she turned and walked away without giving any room for further response. Di Vinci was curious about Sheba, while she saw him as unworthy of her attention.

*The Survivor's Warning*

The next morning, Maximus was summoned to the emperor's chambers, where Centurion Brutus awaited. The soldier's face was pale, his body weakened from his ordeal, but his eyes burned with urgency.

"They will come for you," Brutus said, his voice trembling. "They are not like us. They don't tire. They don't feel fear. And they won't stop until every last man is dead."

Maximus regarded him with a calm intensity. "You survived. What did you see?"

"Death," Brutus replied. "And hunger. They are not human. They are... something else."

"Then we'll show them what it means to face Romans," Maximus said, turning to leave. "Prepare the men. We ride north."

*The Ride North*

By midday, the Seventh Legion was assembled outside the city gates. Soldiers mounted their horses, their armor gleaming in the sunlight. Maximus rode at the head of the column, his mighty men flanking him.

As they set off, the citizens of Rome watched in silence. Some cheered, others whispered prayers, but all understood the gravity of the mission. The riders disappeared into the horizon, their silhouettes fading against the vast expanse of the empire.

Rome had called, and Maximus had answered. But as the wind carried the faint scent of smoke from the north, a question lingered in the air: would they return?

*Ronan...*

Ronan and Maximus share a familial bond—Ronan is

Maximus's younger cousin. Their mothers were sisters, and though they grew up in different villages, they spent their childhood summers together, forging a strong bond. Maximus, always the more disciplined and ambitious of the two, acted as an older brother figure, often encouraging Ronan to focus on honing his skills and rising above his humble beginnings.

While Maximus pursued a career in the Roman legions, Ronan initially stayed behind, content to live a quieter life as a blacksmith and the village protector. His love for steel made him successful, selling his wares in the near and far villages. Despite their different paths, their connection endured through letters, they only saw each other once, when Maximus was camped with the army in a reachable distance.

*The Tragedy of Ronan's Family*

Ronan married Amara, a healer known for her radiant beauty and kind heart. Together, they had a son, Caelus, whose laughter filled their modest home with joy. Ronan believed he had found peace—a life of love and stability. However, peace was shattered when a dark force descended upon their village.

The witch Morwenna, a sorceress feared across Germania for her cruel and twisted magic, targeted Ronan's village. Her motives were unclear, but her actions were devastating. She unleashed a plague of darkness, withering crops, turning livestock into rabid beasts, and driving villagers to madness. Those who resisted her influence met gruesome ends.

Ronan's wife and son were among the casualties. Amara was burned alive by Morwenna's magic as she tried to protect Caelus. The boy, too young to understand what was happening, was taken by Morwenna's minions as a sacrifice. Ronan arrived too late, finding his wife's charred remains and his son's pendant in the ashes.

*The Call to Maximus*

Ronan, consumed by grief and guilt, reached out to Maximus for help. At the time, Maximus was a rising star in the Roman military, commanding respect and authority. Despite his obligations to Rome, Maximus could not ignore Ronan's plea. Their bond ran deeper than blood; they shared a sense of duty to protect those who could not protect themselves.

Maximus arrived in Germania with a small but skilled contingent of soldiers. Upon seeing the devastation in Ronan's village, he vowed to help his cousin find justice. Ronan joined Maximus, leaving behind his forge and vowing to dedicate his life to avenging his family.

*The Two-Year Hunt*

For two years, Ronan and Maximus hunted Morwenna across Germania. The journey tested their resolve, friendship, and faith. They faced countless challenges:

Cursed Forests: Morwenna's magic corrupted the land, creating forests filled with illusions and deadly traps. In one instance, Ronan almost fell victim to a vision of his son calling out to him, but Maximus pulled him back, reminding him of their mission.

Betrayals and Ambushes: Villagers, driven mad by Morwenna's influence, often betrayed the duo, leading them into ambushes set by the witch's minions. Maximus's strategic mind and Ronan's brute strength were the only reasons they survived.

Internal Struggles: Ronan's grief often boiled over into rage, causing him to lash out at Maximus. Despite the tension, Maximus remained patient, understanding that his cousin's pain was driving his actions.

*The Battle in Morwenna's Lair*

The culmination of their hunt brought them to a cave high in the mountains of Germania. The entrance was guarded by grotesque creatures shaped by Morwenna's dark magic—twisted amalgamations of animals and humans. Ronan and Maximus fought their way inside, their bond as warriors stronger than ever.

Inside the lair, they faced Morwenna herself. The witch was a terrifying figure, her eyes glowing with unnatural light and her voice dripping with malice. She unleashed her powers, summoning dark spirits and filling the cave with an oppressive aura. The battle was brutal:

Illusions and Traps: Morwenna conjured visions of Ronan's wife and son, taunting him with the life he had lost. Maximus, unaffected by the illusions, shielded Ronan, giving him the strength to break free from the witch's spell.

The Fight Against Minions: The cave was filled with Morwenna's minions—ghoulish creatures that clawed and bit with unrelenting ferocity. Maximus's tactical mind and Ronan's raw strength allowed them to hold their ground.

A Near-Fatal Encounter: Morwenna's magic struck Maximus with a curse that weakened him, causing him to collapse. Ronan, driven by both rage and love, fought with a fury unmatched, striking down Morwenna's defenses and delivering the final blow.

As Morwenna lay dying, she cursed Ronan, vowing that her darkness would linger in his soul forever. Her words haunted him, even as the cave crumbled around them.

*The Aftermath*

Ronan and Maximus emerged from the cave alive but forever changed. Maximus's curse faded with time, but the physical and emotional toll left scars on both men. Ronan retrieved his wife's pendant from Morwenna's lair, the only tangible reminder of the life he had lost.

Back in Rome, Maximus offered Ronan a place in his legion. Ronan accepted, vowing to serve Maximus with his life. He saw Maximus not just as a leader but as the brother he had never had, the man who had stood by him in his darkest hour.

# 3

# THE JOURNEY NORTH

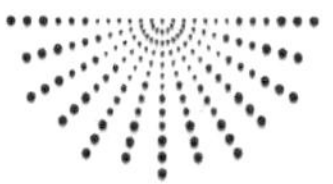

*The Journey Begins*

The week-long journey north tested both the strength and spirit of the Seventh Legion and Senator Di Vinci's personal army. The diverse terrain unfolded like a tapestry of Rome's vast empire: snow-capped mountains rising majestically in the distance, frozen rivers glinting under the winter sun, and dense forests teeming with life. Waterfalls cascaded down jagged cliffs, their roar a constant companion as the armies pushed onward. Vast plains stretched to the horizon, dotted with wildflowers swaying in the cool breeze.

The soldiers moved with precision, their disciplined formations undeterred by the shifting landscapes. At the head of the column, Maximus and Senator Claudius Di Vinci rode side by side, accompanied by General Marcus Lucius Gaius, the commander of Di Vinci's forces. Behind them, Maximus's mighty men marched in silence, their watchful eyes scanning for any signs of danger.

*A Question of Purpose*

On the third day, as they traversed a frozen river, Di Vinci broke the silence. "General Maximus," he began, his tone almost conversational, "I've been meaning to ask: why do you fight for Rome?"

Maximus glanced at him, his expression calm but unreadable. "Because it gives me purpose."

"Purpose?" Di Vinci pressed. "And nothing more? No wealth? No titles? No glory?"

"Glory is fleeting, Senator," Maximus replied. "And wealth makes men weak. Rome is what matters."

General Marcus, riding slightly behind, smirked. "Spoken like a true soldier. But tell me, Maximus, what would you be without Rome?"

Maximus didn't hesitate. "A man. Like any other. But one who chooses his battles wisely."

The mighty men chuckled, but Di Vinci remained contemplative. "And you, Senator?" Conan asked, his tone teasing. "What made you trade silk robes for steel armor?"

Di Vinci's jaw tightened. "Privilege didn't bring me here if that's what you're implying."

"Of course it didn't," Conan said with a grin. "It just rode ahead on a gold-plated chariot."

The group erupted in laughter, but Di Vinci's face darkened. Without a word, he spurred his horse forward, leaving them behind.

. . .

*A Fireside Confession*

That night, as the armies camped at the edge of a dense forest, Di Vinci sat apart from the others, his face illuminated by the flickering flames of the central fire. After a long silence, he began to speak.

"I wasn't born into privilege," he said, his voice steady but tinged with emotion. "My mother and I lived on the streets of old Rome. We begged for food, slept in the cold. She did everything to keep me alive, even... selling herself for a loaf of bread."

The men fell silent, their laughter forgotten.

"She died when I was ten," Di Vinci continued. "Hunger. Sickness. I buried her myself." He paused, his gaze distant. "A kind man took me in after that. Octavius Di Vinci. He gave me his name and a chance at life. But I was still a thief. One day, I was caught, and they were going to take my hand. But Octavius saved me. He brought me into his home, taught me how to be more than I was."

He looked up, his eyes glistening. "I swore I'd make his name great. Not for myself, but for him. That's why I'm here."

Maximus nodded. "The past shapes us all, Senator. But it doesn't define us."


*The Ruins of the Settlements*

The journey continued, and the devastation became increasingly clear. The armies passed through three Roman settlements, each one destroyed beyond recognition. The streets were littered with bodies of both humans and animals, their remains torn apart by something powerful and merciless. The air was thick with the stench of death, and the soldiers moved cautiously, their weapons drawn.

At each site, Maximus ordered the bodies gathered and burned. "We leave no trace of what happened here," he said. "If there's any chance this spreads, we stop it now."

In the second settlement, Han discovered a severed claw. It was twenty inches long, with four fingers ending in razor-sharp tips. The material was hard and heavy, like black stone.

"This isn't from any creature I've ever seen," Han said, showing it to Maximus.

"No," Maximus agreed. "It's something worse."

By the time they reached the third settlement, Aures, the destruction was overwhelming. Buildings lay in ruins, their walls clawed and burned. The soldiers worked tirelessly to gather the remains, their expressions grim. Even Di Vinci struggled to maintain his composure.

The priest approached him, his tone calm but firm. "Courage, Senator. Fear is natural. It reminds us we're alive."

"But for how long?" Di Vinci muttered, his eyes on the distant horizon.

*The Grasslands*

On the seventh day, the armies emerged from the forests into a vast grassland. The open expanse stretched as far as the eye could see, its rolling hills painted with wild-flowers. The soldiers relaxed slightly, the beauty of the scene offering a brief reprieve from the horrors they had witnessed.

Maximus raised his hand, signaling the column to halt. "We make camp here," he announced. "This will be our base."

The soldiers set to work, erecting tents and fortifying the camp. Wooden spikes were driven into the ground, forming a defensive barrier. Wire fences were constructed to deter any potential threats. The mighty men oversaw the preparations, ensuring every detail was accounted for.

*A Strategic Debate*

As the sun dipped below the horizon, General Marcus joined Maximus and his men at the central fire. "We can't afford to wait for them to come to us," Marcus said, his tone firm. "We need to know what's ahead."

Maximus nodded. "What do you propose?"

"I'll send twenty of my best men to scout the surrounding area," Marcus replied. "If there's anything out there, we'll know."

Ronan frowned. "Twenty? Isn't that excessive? We can't afford to lose that many if something goes wrong."

Marcus's gaze was steady. "The threat we face is unlike anything we've known. If caution costs us a few men, it's worth it."

Maximus considered his words, then nodded. "Do it. But make sure they're back by morning."

As Marcus left to organize the scouting party, Ronan leaned toward Maximus. "You trust him?"

"I trust his instincts," Maximus replied. "And his caution. We'll need both."

The camp was quiet that night, the soldiers weary but vigilant. The fires burned low, casting flickering shadows on the grasslands. Somewhere in the darkness, twenty scouts ventured into the unknown, their torches like fireflies against the vast expanse.

Tomorrow, they would learn what lay ahead. But tonight, they fortified their spirits, readying themselves for whatever the dawn might bring.

*Han and Lee...*

The Village of Yuelan:

Han and Lee were born in a remote and serene village named Yuelan, nestled in the mountains of the Far East. The village was renowned for its skilled martial artists, who practiced a unique style of combat, blending agility, precision, and acrobatics. Their parents were among the most respected warriors in Yuelan, having protected the village from raiders and rival clans for years.

The twin brothers were inseparable from birth, often finishing each other's sentences and mirroring each other's movements. While Han was the stockier and more grounded of the two, Lee was lean and nimble, favoring speed over strength. Together, they complemented each other perfectly, often training as a single, unified entity.

Their parents taught them discipline, honor, and the philosophy that strength should only be used to protect the weak. However, their peaceful upbringing came to a brutal end when they were just 15 years old.

*The Fall of Yuelan*

One fateful night, Yuelan was attacked by a ruthless warlord named Kurogai, who sought to enslave the villagers and claim the mountain as his stronghold. Despite the villagers' martial prowess, they were vastly outnumbered. Han and Lee's parents led the resistance, but they were ultimately overwhelmed.

The brothers witnessed their parents' deaths at the hands of Kurogai himself, their sacrifice giving the twins enough time to escape. Clutching a pair of heirloom daggers their parents had gifted them, Han and Lee vowed to one day avenge their village and ensure that no other innocent lives would suffer as theirs had.

*The Wandering Warriors*

For years, Han and Lee wandered the world as mercenaries. They honed their skills, taking on dangerous missions and challenges that others deemed impossible. Their reputation grew, not just for their combat prowess but also for their uncanny ability to work as a single unit. Stories spread of the "Twin Blades of Yuelan," two warriors who moved like shadows and struck with deadly precision.

Despite their fame, the twins remained haunted by their failure to protect their village. They refused to take jobs that involved exploiting or harming innocents, earning them both respect and disdain in the mercenary world. Their ultimate goal remained clear: to gather enough strength and allies to return to Yuelan and overthrow Kurogai.

*Meeting Maximus*

Han and Lee's paths crossed with Maximus during a mission in the city of Arelia, a bustling port town in the Roman Empire. Maximus and his men had been hired to protect the city from a band of raiders who were threatening to cut off its vital trade routes. Unknown to Maximus, Han and Lee had also been hired by the city's merchant guild for the same reason.

The raiders attacked under the cover of night, their numbers far greater than anyone had anticipated. During the battle, Maximus and his mighty men found themselves overwhelmed and surrounded. Just as defeat seemed inevitable, Han and Lee appeared, their twin blades slicing through the raiders with unmatched speed and precision.

The twins' arrival turned the tide of the battle. Their ability to coordinate with Maximus's men without prior communication amazed everyone. By dawn, the raiders were defeated, and the city was saved.

*Joining the Mighty Men*

After the battle, Maximus approached the twins, impressed by their skill and honor. He invited them to join his band of warriors, offering them a chance to fight for a greater purpose.

At first, Han and Lee were hesitant. They were lone wolves, accustomed to working on their own terms. But Maximus's charisma and unwavering sense of justice resonated with them. He reminded them of their parents' teachings and offered something they hadn't felt in years: a sense of belonging.

The twins eventually accepted, but with one condition: Maximus would one day help them reclaim Yuelan and bring Kurogai to justice. Maximus agreed, seeing their cause as noble and aligned with his own values.

*Life with the Mighty Men*

Han and Lee quickly became indispensable members of Maximus's mighty men. Their agility and stealth made them ideal for reconnaissance and surprise attacks, while their teamwork inspired the rest of the group.

Han earned a reputation for his resilience and unshakable focus in the heat of battle, while Lee became known for his daring acrobatics and deadly precision. Together, they were a force to be reckoned with, their bond unbreakable even in the face of overwhelming odds.

While they never forgot their ultimate goal, Han and Lee found a new family among Maximus's men. The camaraderie and shared purpose gave them a renewed sense of hope, and they vowed to fight not just for Yuelan but for the ideals Maximus and his warriors represented.

*Foreshadowing Their Return to Yuelan*

As the story progresses, Han and Lee's past and their vow to reclaim Yuelan become central to their character arcs. Their relationship with Maximus deepens, and the group's adventures bring them closer to confronting Kurogai and the ghosts of their past.

*It's time*

Years after joining Maximus's mighty men, Han and Lee finally saw their chance to fulfill the vow they had made to their parents and their village. After a particularly grueling campaign, Maximus noticed the twins sitting apart from the group, their normally light-hearted demeanor replaced by a rare seriousness.

"What troubles you?" Maximus asked, his voice calm yet commanding.

Han spoke first, his tone uncharacteristically grave. "It's time, General. We've fought beside you for years, but we can no longer delay. We must reclaim Yuelan."

Lee added, "Our village is still under the rule of Kurogai. Every day that monster lives, our people suffer."

Maximus placed a firm hand on Han's shoulder. "You've given everything for us, for Rome. It's time we return the favor."

With Maximus's unwavering support, the mighty men prepared for a campaign unlike any other. The journey to Yuelan was long and perilous, but their bond and shared sense of justice carried them forward. For Han and Lee, this was more than a battle—it was the culmination of years of grief, pain, and determination.

· · ·

*The Battle for Yuelan*

When the group reached the outskirts of Yuelan, they were met with a somber sight. The once-thriving village was a shadow of its former self, its walls crumbling, its fields barren, and its people downtrodden. Kurogai's forces, however, were formidable, their presence marked by an army of ruthless warriors and mercenaries.

Maximus, ever the strategist, devised a plan to divide and conquer Kurogai's forces. Han and Lee led a group to infiltrate the village under the cover of darkness, freeing captives and rallying the villagers to their cause. Meanwhile, Maximus and the rest of his mighty men launched a surprise attack on the enemy camp, drawing Kurogai's forces into a decisive confrontation.

The battle was fierce and chaotic. Han and Lee fought with a fury born of years of pent-up rage and sorrow. Their twin blades moved with unparalleled speed and precision, cutting through Kurogai's men as if guided by fate itself. Maximus, Conan, Lugo, and the others held the line, their combined strength and tactics turning the tide of the battle.

Finally, the confrontation reached its climax in Kurogai's stronghold. Han and Lee faced the warlord in a brutal duel. Kurogai, a towering figure clad in dark armor, was no ordinary opponent. His strikes were powerful and unrelenting, his sheer strength pushing the twins to their limits.

But Han and Lee fought as one, their movements perfectly synchronized. When Kurogai swung his massive blade at Han, Lee struck from behind, creating an opening for his brother. Together, they delivered the final blow, ending the warlord's reign of terror.

. . .

*The People's Plea*

With Kurogai defeated, the people of Yuelan emerged from their homes, their expressions a mixture of awe and gratitude. The elders of the village approached Han and Lee, their voices trembling with emotion.

"You have done what we thought impossible," said the eldest among them. "You have avenged your parents and restored hope to our village. It is only fitting that you lead us, as your parents once did."

The villagers knelt before the twins, their collective plea echoing through the square. "Lead us, protect us, guide us as you were destined to."

Han and Lee exchanged a long glance, their hearts heavy with the weight of the decision. This was everything they had dreamed of, everything their parents had wanted for them. Yet, they knew their journey was not over.

*The Oath of Loyalty*

That night, Han and Lee spoke with Maximus, their faces etched with conflict.

"We owe them our lives," Han began, his voice thick with emotion. "This is what we've fought for."

Lee nodded. "But our duty, our loyalty, is to you. You gave us purpose when we had nothing. You taught us to fight for more than just vengeance."

Maximus regarded them silently for a moment before

speaking. "Your people need you. You've earned the right to stay and rebuild. You don't owe me anything."

Han shook his head firmly. "We owe you everything. If you hadn't believed in us, we wouldn't be here today. Yuelan will always be our home, but we cannot abandon you now."

The next day, before the entire village, the soldiers assembled to leave, and the villagers and the twins came up. "I know you will protect and serve your people well as you have served with us." His voice was heavy. Lee added, "Our parents taught us that honor lies in loyalty and sacrifice. We choose to follow you, General. Wherever you go, we go."

Han and Lee swore an oath to Maximus, a bond that would define their lives. They knelt before him, their voices steady and resolute.

"We, Han and Lee, sons of Yuelan, pledge our lives to General Maximus. In battle and in peace, we will stand by your side until death takes us."

The villagers, though saddened by the twins' departure, understood their choice. The elders named new leaders, ensuring that Yuelan would remain protected and prosperous.

*A Legacy of Honor*

As they left Yuelan, Han and Lee carried with them not just the memories of their parents and their village, but also the knowledge that they had fulfilled their promise. They had avenged their family, freed their people, and restored honor to their name.

For Maximus and the mighty men, Han and Lee's loyalty was a testament to the unbreakable bonds forged in battle. Together, they would face whatever challenges lay ahead, knowing that their shared purpose and unwavering trust would guide them through even the darkest of times.

Their journey serves as a powerful reminder that even the most skilled warriors are shaped by their losses and that true strength lies not just in combat but in the bonds they form and the causes they fight for.

4

# THE ENCOUNTER

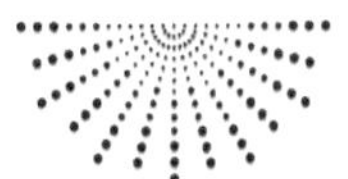

*The Watchtower's Alarm*

By noon, the camp was bustling with activity. Soldiers sharpened weapons, fortified defenses, and prepared for what lay ahead. The watchtower stood tall, manned by two guards scanning the horizon.

The younger guard squinted into the distance, his hand shielding his eyes from the sun. "Do you see that?" he asked.

The older guard raised his spyglass. A group of riders emerged from the horizon—seven of the twenty scouts who had left that morning. They were galloping at full speed, their movements frantic.

"Something's wrong," the older guard muttered. Then he saw them.

Behind the riders, three massive creatures bounded across the grasslands. Standing between ten and twelve feet tall, with tar-black skin glinting in the sunlight, they moved

43

with terrifying speed. Their hulking bodies were covered in scales as hard as steel, and their massive claws tore into the ground with each leap. Slime dripped from their wide, fanged jaws as guttural roars echoed across the plains.

"They're coming!" the guard shouted, grabbing the alarm bell and ringing it with all his might. The sound reverberated through the camp, sending soldiers scrambling to their positions.

The seven riders reached the camp just as the creatures closed in. One of the scouts blew his horn, signaling the danger. But before they could reach safety, the beasts struck.

The first creature leapt, bringing down a horse and its rider with a single swipe. The scout's screams were drowned out by the beast's deafening roar. Another scout tried to veer away, but the second creature caught his horse mid-stride, ripping it apart with terrifying ease.

The soldiers at the camp's edge stood frozen in shock, watching as the creatures tore through men and horses alike. Finally, the officers barked orders, and two hundred of Di Vinci's men charged into the field.

The battle began in chaos. Swords and spears glanced off the creatures' armored hides, their blows doing little more than enraging the beasts. The creatures swung their massive claws, sending men and horses flying through the air. Green slime sprayed as the beasts tore through the soldiers, their ferocity unmatched.

*Maximus and His Mighty Men*

Hearing the commotion, Maximus and his mighty men mounted their horses. "Form up!" Maximus commanded, his voice cutting through the chaos.

They rode into the fray, their weapons gleaming in the sunlight. The first creature fell to their combined assault, its scaled hide pierced by Ronan's sword and Sheba's whip. Han and Lee darted around the second beast, their knives finding weak spots in its joints. Lugo's mighty axe cleaved into the third creature's leg, bringing it to its knees.

Di Vinci, though pale with fear, charged into the battle. His sword swung wildly as he aimed for the third beast. The creature fell, its massive body crashing down, but not before pinning Di Vinci beneath it.

"Is he dead?" Ronan asked, dismounting and rushing to Di Vinci's side.

Sheba laughed despite the chaos. "No, he's still fighting his way out."

Di Vinci emerged from beneath the creature, covered in slime but unharmed. "You better believe it," he said, his voice shaking but defiant. "I came here to make the name Di Vinci great, and I intend to do just that."

Maximus smirked. "I was going to write on your tombstone: Here lies Di Vinci, slain by a dead monster. But I guess you'll live to fight another day."

The soldiers cheered as the last of the creatures fell, their massive forms lifeless on the blood-soaked field.

*The Nameless One Speaks*

As the camp settled, Maximus retreated to his tent, washing the green blood from his armor. His nameless slave entered hesitantly.

"Master, I beg permission to speak."

"Speak," Maximus said, not looking up.

The slave hesitated. "I would congratulate you on the victory, but I'm afraid it means nothing."

Maximus frowned, finally meeting the slave's gaze. "What do you mean?"

"These creatures," the slave continued, his voice steady despite the weight of his words, "were newly hatched. There are thousands more. And they will not stop until all men are dead."

Maximus's expression darkened. "How do you know this?"

The slave hesitated, then spoke quietly. "Because I've seen them before."

Before Maximus could question him further, the alarm horn sounded again. Maximus rushed to the camp's edge, where Lee pointed toward the horizon.

Fifty creatures, larger and more fearsome than the first three, were advancing toward the camp.

*Preparing for the Next Battle*

Maximus turned to his men, his voice calm but firm. "Conan, organize the defense. Ronan, get the archers in position. Sheba, flank them from the left. Han and Lee, stay close to me."

Di Vinci approached, his armor freshly polished. "What about me, General?"

"You'll take your men and flank from the right," Maximus said. "But only on my signal. We hold the line until then."

As the soldiers formed ranks, Maximus drew his sword. "We fight as Romans," he said, his voice rising above the noise. "We fight as one."

The soldiers roared in response, their fear replaced with determination.

As the creatures closed in, their roars echoing across the plains, Maximus whispered to himself, "May the gods be with us."

The battle that followed would test the strength, courage, and unity of the soldiers. But even as the first wave of arrows rained down on the approaching beasts, one truth became clear: the war against these creatures was only just beginning.

The chaos outside the tent was deafening—the clash of steel, the screams of soldiers, and the roars of the monstrous Kiballangu echoed across the battlefield. Inside the dimly lit tent, Maximus sat on a makeshift chair, sweat dripping from his brow, his leg freshly bandaged but visibly broken. His breathing was labored, the pain barely masked by his stoic demeanor. The slave knelt before him, quietly cleaning the blood-stained swords Maximus had discarded.

Maximus looked at the slave, his voice strained. "How bad is it out there?"

The slave hesitated. "It is worse than you think, Master. The men… they are dying faster than the creatures can kill them."

Maximus's jaw tightened. He looked away, anger flashing in his eyes. "They are fighting to the last breath. That's what soldiers do. We've faced worse."

The slave's voice softened but carried a weight of urgency. "No, Master, you have not faced worse. This is not a battle you can win."

Maximus turned to him sharply. "What are you saying? Are you trying to break my resolve?"

The slave lowered his gaze but pressed on. "Master, I speak only the truth. You lost two hundred men to just three of these creatures. Now, there are fifty out there, and more will come. If you do not stop this now, they will devour all of us."

Maximus's tone hardened. "Enough. You are my slave, not my advisor. I do not need your counsel. What I need is for you to stay silent and let me think."

The slave, visibly nervous but resolute, stood up. "Master, you do not have much time. You must leave. Ride to your wife and son. Take them across the great sea. Run, Master. Keep running because these creatures will not stop until every last man is dead."

Maximus slammed his fist onto the table, his frustration boiling over. "You dare tell me to run? Have I ever run from a battle? Have I not been kind to you, allowed you to serve under the greatest general Rome has ever seen?"

The slave's voice grew firmer, though still respectful. "Master, you are a great general. But greatness cannot stop death. These creatures are not mere beasts—they are the beginning of an end you cannot fight alone."

Maximus leaned forward, his voice low but trembling with restrained anger. "You speak of the end? Then tell me how to stop it. If you have the wisdom of the gods, share it. Otherwise, hold your tongue."

The slave met his gaze, a flicker of desperation in his eyes. "I can stop them, Master. But only if you free me."

### The Request for Freedom

Maximus blinked, stunned by the audacity of the request. "What did you just say?"

The slave stood straighter now, his voice calm but unyielding. "I said, free me, Master. I cannot do what must be done while I am bound by chains."

Maximus stared at him, incredulous. "You want freedom now? In the middle of this madness? You think freedom will suddenly make you capable of killing fifty of these monsters?"

The slave nodded. "It is not freedom alone. You must give me something to symbolize my freedom. A token of your trust, something that shows the world I am no longer bound."

Maximus shook his head, exasperated. "This is absurd. What do you want—a medal? My cloak? Gold?"

The slave's gaze fell to Maximus's neck, where a medallion hung. "That medallion will do."

Maximus clutched it instinctively. "This? This is a gift from my father. It is no mere trinket."

The slave's voice grew softer. "And what good will it do you if you're dead, Master? You need me to save your men, your family, and Rome itself. Give me the medallion, and I will give you a chance to win."

Maximus stared at him for a long moment, his anger fading into a begrudging understanding. He removed the medallion, holding it out reluctantly. "Take it. But if you fail, this will be the last thing I ever give you."

The slave took the medallion and placed it around his neck. As it touched his skin, a faint light pulsed through his body. Maximus recoiled slightly. "What in the gods' name was that?"

The slave smiled faintly. "The beginning of my freedom."

*The Swords*

The slave stepped toward the table where Maximus's swords lay. "There is one more thing, Master. I need your titanium swords."

Maximus groaned, his patience fraying. "Must I tell you everything? Take the swords and stop wasting time."

The slave picked up the swords, their weight familiar in his hands. He closed his eyes, muttering words under his breath. "Swords to hands, hands to swords, let the enemies that defy my land fall where they stand."

A sudden gust of wind tore through the tent, extinguishing the lamps. Maximus shielded his face, his eyes wide as the slave—no, the Freeman—stood bathed in a faint glow.

"What have I done?" Maximus whispered.


*The Battlefield*

Outside, the soldiers were retreating, the creatures tearing through their ranks with terrifying precision. The Freeman stepped out, his presence halting the fleeing men. His voice boomed across the battlefield.

"Blow the horn of retreat!" he commanded.

Maximus hesitated but obeyed, the sound of the horn echoing through the valley. The soldiers began to pull back, confused but relieved.

The Freeman stepped forward, his swords gleaming. "Let them come," he muttered.

And they did. The fifty Kiballangu rushed toward him, their massive forms blotting out the horizon. The soldiers watched in stunned silence as the Freeman charged headlong into the fray.

His movements were a blur, his swords slicing through the creatures with ease. Limbs fell, and green slime sprayed into the air as he tore through the horde. When his swords became lodged in one creature's chest, he switched to his bare hands, ripping another beast apart limb by limb.

The soldiers, frozen in awe, could only watch as the Freeman single-handedly pushed the Kiballangu back into the woods. The remaining creatures, now fewer than five, fled into the darkness, their roars fading into the distance.

.  .  .

*The Freeman's Revelation*

When the Freeman returned to the camp, the soldiers parted for him, their faces a mixture of fear and awe. He approached Maximus, who sat in stunned silence. The Freeman poured water over himself, washing away the blood and slime, before sitting down beside the general.

"We need to talk," the Freeman said simply.

Maximus nodded slowly. "I don't even know where to begin. What are you? What did I just witness?"

The Freeman looked at him, his expression calm but serious. "I am from another world. I am one of seven Guardians tasked with protecting the balance of all realms. But I lost my name, and with it, my full power."

Maximus frowned. "Your name? What does that have to do with anything?"

"My name is my essence," the Freeman explained. "Without it, I am incomplete. The mother of these creatures holds the energy of my name. If I can retrieve it, I can stop them."

Maximus leaned forward. "Then we retrieve it. What do you need?"

"A small team," the Freeman said. "More men will only mean more deaths. And you, General, must be the one to name me."

Maximus blinked. "Why me?"

"Because you gave me my freedom," the Freeman said simply. "And only the one who freed me can give me my name."

Maximus stared at him, the weight of the moment sinking in. "Then let's get your name back. For all our sakes.

# MY WORLD

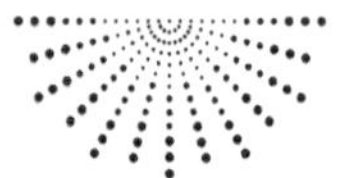

The campfire crackled softly in the stillness of the night, its embers rising and disappearing into the cool mountain air. The team sat around it, their faces illuminated in flickering shadows. They were exhausted after three days of travel, chasing waterfalls and battling the relentless terrain. Nameless sat apart, his expression distant and contemplative, as if seeing something beyond their world.

Sheba and Di Vinci were locked in a heart-to-heart conversation. "You're wrong, Sheba. People don't need families to leave a legacy. They need courage—and you have plenty of that."

Sheba (softly): "Maybe you're not as useless as I thought."

Finally, Nameless broke the silence. "In my world," he began, his voice low but commanding, "warriors are more plentiful than common men. Every corner of our civilization breathes the essence of strength and duty. We are not like this world. Ours is a realm of advanced beauty and boundless potential yet steeped in tradition and responsibility."

The others leaned in closer, drawn by the richness of his words.

"My world is called High Sky," he continued, "a land of shimmering towers that pierce the heavens. Our streets are paved with stones that radiate light, and our bridges are spun from pure energy, connecting realms and minds alike. Water flows through our cities, singing a melody that harmonizes with the very air we breathe. Beauty and function coexist in ways you cannot fathom. But above all, High Sky is a world ruled by women, for it was the woman who was first created by the light. They are our leaders, protectors, and the foundation of our society."

He paused, his gaze shifting to the flickering flames. "Our traditions are sacred. Every fifty nights, the Day of Choosing is held. It is a day when the women—our leaders, warriors, and healers—choose their mates. Men do not decide; they are chosen, and that is how it has always been. The ceremony is one of both honor and humility."

Nameless's tone grew heavier as he delved deeper into his tale. "On one such Day of Choosing, the head of the high council's daughter was ready to select her mate. Her name was Mahananu, and she was the most beautiful woman in all of High Sky. She resided in the highest of towers, a place where only the Guardians and Council lived. Her beauty was legendary, so much so that no Guardian dared to stand before her—including my brother, the Red Guardian. But I, the Blue Guardian, found myself chosen by her. Prior to that special day, we, Guardians, wished she would pick one of us, but the Red Guardian was certain it would be him. The maiden that chose the Red Guardian, was believed to have spoilt the selection of Mahananu's choosing of the Red Guardian. Once chosen, you are committed till death."

The camp fell silent, the weight of his words settling over them. Nameless continued, his voice tinged with sorrow. "My brother's heart was shattered that day. He had hoped—believed—that she would choose him. But instead, she chose me. That choice was the beginning of his descent into darkness. Hatred festered within him, feeding on his heartbreak and growing like a cancer. He began to tap into forbidden powers, fueled by his anger. His strength grew, his brain power surpassing what even I could achieve, but it came at a cost. He broke his commitment to his maiden, neglecting her in his obsession. Then one day, she was found dead."

Nameless's voice cracked, the pain of old memories surfacing. "When she died, he sought out Mahananu. He told her he had done it for her—that they could be together now. He even offered to kill me, so they could flee to another realm. But Mahananu, with her unshakable resolve, turned him away. She told him she would rather die than be with him. So, he killed her."

The team exchanged uneasy glances, but no one spoke. Nameless pressed on, his voice hardening. "When I returned home, I found her gone. My brother had taken her body to a place only he knew. Our laws demanded that I bring him back to face Septigonu Judgment, but my culture demanded blood. The honor of the Blue Guardian demanded retribution. I set out to find him, tracking him across realms. My journey led me here, to your world, but not before I lost everything—including my name. Without a name, I am incomplete, a shadow of the man I once was."

Di Vinci, ever curious, leaned forward. "You said your world is advanced, yet you speak of honor and tradition as if they outweigh technology. Why?"

Nameless regarded him with a faint smile. "Because honor is what binds us. Without it, advancement becomes chaos. A blade in the hands of the dishonorable is destruction; a blade in the hands of the honorable is salvation. In High Sky, our strength lies in our people, not just our technology. Our traditions guide us, keep us from losing ourselves to power."

He shifted, his expression softening. "And then there are the Protectors—warriors who can access thirty percent of their brain power. It is a gift that allows them to perform incredible feats: enhanced strength, accelerated healing, and the ability to manipulate energy. Yet, even among the Protectors, there are the Guardians of the Realm. Seven of us, each representing a color that embodies our essence. I was the Blue Guardian—calm and wise. My brother, the Red Guardian, was passionate and powerful. Together with the others—Green, Black, Brown, Yellow, and the White Guardian, who leads us—we were the defenders of our realm."

He looked around the group, his expression turning grave. "But not all Guardians remain pure. To be a Guardian, one must access seventy percent of their brain power. Failure to do so leads to exile—to the Lost Grounds of Laladaru, where only madness awaits. My brother... he was not exiled. Instead, he chose to walk a darker path, one that threatens to consume everything I hold dear."

The team sat in silence, the weight of his words pressing down on them. Nameless's tale was more than a story; it was a glimpse into a world of unimaginable beauty and tragedy—a world teetering on the edge of collapse.

As the fire crackled and the group gathered their breath after the tale of the Red Guardian's betrayal, Di Vinci asked, "What you've told us about your world is fascinating, Nameless. But you've spoken of Protectors, Guardians, and council maidens—what are the structures that hold High Sky together? Who governs this place of power and beauty?"

Nameless looked into the flames, his face illuminated by the glow, and nodded. "Our world thrives on order, and that order is maintained through layers of leadership, each with distinct roles and responsibilities. The highest level of governance is the Council of Light, a group of seven women chosen for their wisdom, strength, and connection to the essence of our realm. They are not just leaders; they are the custodians of the light that birthed High Sky. They guide us with laws that balance advancement and tradition, ensuring that power never becomes our undoing.

"Beneath the Council of Light are the Matriarchs of the Realms. These are leaders of specific regions within High Sky, and their authority is absolute within their territories. Matriarchs are warriors as well as rulers, chosen for their ability to lead in battle and diplomacy alike. Each Matriarch commands a legion of Protectors who serve as their enforcers and guardians. However, even the Matriarchs must answer to the Council of Light in matters of significant importance."

He paused, taking a deep breath. "And then there are the Guardians of the Realm, the seven of us who serve as the ultimate protectors of High Sky. While the Matriarchs govern and the Protectors enforce, the Guardians are the final shield against threats that would destroy everything. We are not bound by the territories of the Matriarchs; our duty is to the entire realm. The White Guardian, who is the leader of the Guardians, serves as the bridge between us and the Council of Light. She carries their will and ensures that we act in accordance with the realm's greater good."

Nameless's gaze became distant as he spoke of the Guardians. "Each of us represents a force, a color that embodies our essence. The White Guardian, the most powerful of us all, is the embodiment of balance and purity. The Red Guardian, my brother, was the force of passion and war. The Green Guardian represents growth and healing, while the Black Guardian embodies mystery and strategy. The Yellow Guardian channels energy and light, the Brown Guardian symbolizes resilience and earth, and I, the Blue Guardian, represent calm and wisdom. Together, we were meant to be an unstoppable force, a harmony that no enemy could break."

Di Vinci, ever the skeptic, leaned forward. "You speak as if your world is flawless, but power corrupts. Surely, there must be struggles even in High Sky."

Nameless's jaw tightened. "Flawless? No. We have our

flaws, our battles. The Council of Light, for all their wisdom, are not immune to disagreements, nor are the Matriarchs free from ambition. But what keeps us together is the understanding that our survival depends on unity. And yet, my brother is proof that even unity has its limits. His fall is a stain on all of us, a reminder that power, unchecked by honor, is a curse."

He turned to the rest of the group, his voice softening. "There is one more layer of leadership I have not spoken of: the Chosen Maidens. These women are selected by the Council to act as advisers and emissaries, serving as the voice of the people. They are not warriors or rulers but are often more powerful than both. Their insight and intuition shape the decisions of the Council and the Matriarchs. It was among these maidens that Mahananu rose, her wisdom and beauty unmatched. It is said that the light itself wept when she was taken from us."

The group fell silent, the weight of Nameless's words settling over them. The world he described was a place of staggering complexity, a society built on layers of leadership and bound by traditions that balanced progress with honor.

"But," Nameless continued, his tone darkening, "all of this—our towers, our laws, our Guardians—means nothing without the light. The light is the source of all life in High Sky, and it is dying. My brother's actions and my failure to stop him have weakened it. Without the light, our world will crumble, just as surely as this fire will die without fuel. I am the sin of a namer, and it is with pride I wear my color. There are only seven guardians, as there are seven provinces, seven matriarchs, and seven high council members," he spoke as his hope increased.

"What is a namer?", Di Vinci asked...

"These are special kind of people, gifted with the ability to name every thing they find," he replied.

The flames flickered lower, as if punctuating his point. The team sat in silence, their thoughts racing. Di Vinci finally spoke. "And yet, you are here, Nameless, fighting a different battle. Why? Why not return to High Sky and save your world?"

Nameless stared into the fire, his expression unreadable. "Because my name is the key to everything. Without it, I cannot return. Without it, I am no longer the Blue Guardian—I am just a shadow of what I was. And here, in this world, I believe I will find it. My brother left clues for me, trails meant to torment me. But they are also my only hope. If I can reclaim my name, I can return to High Sky and face him. Until then, I fight here, among you, to keep my skills sharp and my purpose alive."

The fire burned low as the group prepared for sleep. Nameless's story lingered in their minds, a haunting reminder of the beauty and fragility of a world they could only imagine. As they drifted off, one thought prevailed: Nameless was not just a warrior or a leader—he was a man caught between two worlds, bound by a duty that transcended them both.

The fire crackled softly as the group listened intently to Nameless. His voice remained steady, but there was an undercurrent of pain as he continued his tale.

"The law of my world demands that I bring my brother,

the Red Guardian, back to face Septigonu Judgment. It is the ultimate trial, reserved for the gravest of crimes, and the outcome is always the same—justice, swift and unyielding. But my culture... my culture requires something different. It demands blood for blood. To restore the honor of the Guardians, I must end his life myself. These conflicting duties weigh heavily on me, but in truth, neither is possible until I find him."

Nameless paused, his gaze fixed on the flickering flames. "I followed him across realms, driven by the clues he left behind. It was his twisted game, designed to torment me. But crossing into a foreign realm is no simple task. In my world, for a Guardian to step into another realm, their name must precede them. The name carries our essence, our identity. It goes first, paving the way for us to follow. But when I arrived here, I found that my name was missing —stolen, taken from me. Without it, I am incomplete, a shadow of what I once was."

He clenched his fists, his voice thick with anger and sorrow. "I searched everywhere, following every whisper, every lead, but it was all in vain. And then... I fell into the hands of slave traders. They saw me not as a warrior, not as a Guardian, but as something to be sold. They gave me food to keep me alive, only to sell me into slavery. It was the ultimate humiliation, yet it also gave me clarity. My brother's betrayal had brought me here, stripped me of my name and my purpose. But it had not broken me."

The group sat in stunned silence, absorbing the weight of his words. Finally, Di Vinci spoke, his curiosity piqued. "You've spoken of incredible power—how much of it are you using now, Nameless? And can we learn to do the same?"

Nameless's lips curved into a faint, humorless smile. "I am using as much as a Protector. That is why I can heal quickly, why I can fight with the precision and strength you've seen. But it is only a fraction of what I could once wield as a Guardian. As for whether you can learn... that depends."

The group leaned in, eager to hear more. Nameless gestured for them to listen carefully. "Your minds are like doors. Most of you keep those doors closed, afraid of what lies beyond. To access more of your brain power, you must first open those doors and face what you fear. It is not just a matter of will but of discipline and understanding."

He paused, studying their faces. "To use thirty percent of your brain power, as the Protectors do, is no small feat. It requires years of training, intense focus, and an unshakable resolve. But to reach seventy percent, the level of a Guardian? That is something only a chosen few can achieve. It is not just about strength—it is about balance, about harmony within oneself."

He attempted to explain further, describing techniques for channeling energy and unlocking potential. But as he spoke, frustration began to brew among his companions.

"This isn't making any sense," one of them muttered, throwing up their hands in exasperation.

Another shook their head. "It sounds like riddles. How are we supposed to open doors in our minds? What does that even mean?"

Nameless sighed, his expression weary. "You lack the

patience to understand. You want power without the discipline to wield it. That is why I am a Guardian, and you are not."

The conversation dissolved into muttered complaints, but Nameless remained unfazed. He turned his attention back to the fire, his thoughts drifting once more to his brother and the path that lay ahead.

After the fireplace was deserted, Han and Lee sat by the fire, polishing their blades. The group rested after a grueling journey.

Han (grinning): "Do you remember the elder's lessons? He said our blades should cut with the precision of our hearts."

Lee (dryly): "And then you chopped down half the training dummies."

Han (laughing): "I was aiming for precision. Strength was a bonus."

They share a laugh, but their mood turns somber as they glance at the distant mountains.

Han: "Lee… if something happens, promise me you'll finish the fight."

Lee (firmly placing a hand on his brother's shoulder, with steady eyes a a firm tone): "You're my brother. Nothing will happen to you unless it happens to me first."

Their bond was palpable

Di Vinci was sitting with Maximus, staring at a map of the enemy's position.

Di Vinci (quietly): "When I left Rome, I was chasing glory. I thought that was the legacy my children would remember me for."

Maximus (curious): "And now?"

Di Vinci: "Now I see it's not about glory. It's about doing what must be done. Even if no one remembers."

Maximus studied him, a faint respect growing in his expression. Ronan and Conan shared a glance outside the tent, for they heard the conversation. Conan shrugged, while Ronan rolled his eyes. "Please," Said Ronan.

*The Hunt Resumes*

After several failed attempts to locate the mother Gremor, the group reached a resting point near a towering waterfall. The sound of rushing water filled the air, mingling with the rustling of leaves in the small forest that bordered the flowing river. Nameless, ever alert, suddenly tensed.

"We are not alone," he said quietly, his voice cutting through the ambient noise. "The Gremors are close."

The group froze, their hands instinctively reaching for their weapons. Nameless motioned for everyone to stay calm. "Conan," he said, gesturing toward the mountain overlooking the falls, "come with me. The rest of you, stay here and remain vigilant."

The two of them climbed the rocky slope, their steps cautious but swift. When they reached the summit, Conan scanned the area, his sharp eyes searching for any sign of movement.

"I don't see anything," he said, his voice laced with doubt.

Nameless, however, remained focused. He unsheathed

his swords and walked toward a large boulder shaped suspiciously like an egg. "The unique thing about the Gremors," he began, his voice calm, "is their ability to change color to match their surroundings. They can blend perfectly into the environment, but there is one thing they cannot hide—the sound of their hearts."

With a swift, decisive strike, Nameless plunged his sword into the boulder. A deafening scream erupted as the Gremor revealed itself, its camouflage failing. The creature thrashed wildly, its massive form towering over them.

Three more Gremors uncloaked, their monstrous figures emerging from the surrounding rocks and foliage. Conan reacted quickly, severing the claws of one with a powerful swing of his blade. He leaped onto its back, stabbing relentlessly as it thrashed and swayed. The creature stumbled toward the edge of the cliff and plummeted into the river below, but Conan followed, sword in hand.

From the water's edge, he continued his assault, slashing at the emerging Gremor as it tried to climb onto the rocks. Meanwhile, Nameless fought with a controlled ferocity, dispatching the remaining creatures on the mountaintop with precision strikes.

When the battle ended, the group regrouped near the base of the falls. Their faces were grim, their breaths heavy.

Nameless wiped the blood from his blades and turned to the others. "This was only a skirmish. The mother Gremor is still out there, and she will not be as easily defeated. We must be prepared for what lies ahead."

The team nodded, their resolve hardened. As they resumed their journey, the weight of Nameless's story and the dangers of their mission hung heavily over them. The path ahead was uncertain, but one thing was clear: their survival depended on understanding not only their enemy but also themselves.

*Sheba...*

The Jewel of Luxor

Sheba was once a celebrated warrior-princess of Luxor, a powerful city nestled along the Nile. Known for her unmatched skill with the whip-sword and her sharp, strategic mind, she was both admired and feared. Her beauty was legendary, her name synonymous with grace and strength, and her people revered her as a protector and leader.

Luxor flourished under her command, its people enjoying peace and prosperity. Sheba's life seemed destined for greatness—until betrayal shattered everything she held dear.

*The Fall of Luxor*

In her twenty-fifth year, Luxor was betrayed from within. A trusted general, driven by greed and jealousy, opened the city's gates to an invading force of desert marauders. The once-mighty defenses of Luxor crumbled under the onslaught, and the city was plunged into chaos.

Sheba fought valiantly, her whip-sword slicing through the invaders with deadly precision. But even her extraordinary skill was not enough to turn the tide. The marauders overran the city, slaughtering its people and setting its grand temples ablaze. Sheba's family—her father, the Pharaoh, her mother, and her younger brother—were executed before her eyes.

Captured and bound, Sheba was paraded through the streets of her burning city. Her spirit, however, remained unbroken. "You may take my kingdom," she spat at her captors, "but you will never take my soul."

The invaders, unwilling to kill such a fierce and defiant woman, sold her into slavery. Stripped of her titles and dignity, Sheba was forced to fight in gladiatorial pits across the Mediterranean, her skills used for the entertainment of the cruel and powerful.

### The Gladiator's Curse

For years, Sheba endured the brutality of the arenas. She became a favorite among the crowds, her whip-sword dancing with deadly beauty. But her victories brought no solace; each fight was a reminder of all she had lost.

Despite the despair that threatened to consume her, Sheba held onto a spark of hope. She vowed that one day, she would regain her freedom and avenge her family and her city. That hope sustained her, even as the chains of her captors grew heavier.

### Maximus's Intervention

Sheba's life took an unexpected turn when she was

brought to Rome to compete in one of the empire's grandest arenas. Her reputation had preceded her, and the crowds eagerly awaited the "Queen of the Sands" to showcase her deadly skill.

Among the spectators that day was General Maximus, accompanied by his early band of mighty men—Han, Lee, Conan, and Onan. They had come to Rome to rally support for a campaign, but Maximus's attention was drawn to the fierce warrior in the pit.

He watched as Sheba fought with a ferocity and grace that reminded him of the warriors he had led into battle. But he also saw the pain in her eyes, the weight of loss and betrayal that drove her every move. When the match ended, and Sheba stood victorious but bloodied, Maximus made a decision.

Later that night, Maximus visited the arena's holding cells, where Sheba and the other gladiators were kept. With the gold and influence he had gained from his campaigns, he negotiated her freedom. Sheba, though suspicious of his motives, agreed to accompany him, if only to escape the chains that had bound her for so long.

*Earning Her Place*

At first, Sheba was wary of Maximus and his companions. She had trusted before, and it had cost her everything. But as they traveled together, she began to see that Maximus was different. He treated her as an equal, valuing her skills and insights. Han and Lee, initially skeptical of her, grew to admire her prowess with the whip-sword. Conan, with his gruff demeanor, respected her fiery spirit.

Ronan, ever the silent observer, was the first to recognize the depth of Sheba's pain. One night, as the group camped by a river, he approached her and spoke softly. "You carry the weight of a kingdom lost. But you are more than your past. With Maximus, we fight not just for glory but for redemption."

Sheba's journey to trust and belonging was not easy. She clashed with Conan over leadership decisions, sparred with Han and Lee to prove her worth, and often challenged Maximus's strategies. But with every battle they fought together, her walls began to crumble.

In one particularly harrowing mission, the group was ambushed by mercenaries. When Sheba's whip-sword was knocked from her hand, she fought with nothing but her bare hands, protecting Han and Lee from harm. It was at that moment that she earned the full respect and loyalty of the group.

One evening, as the group rested after a victorious campaign, Sheba approached Maximus by the fire. Her expression was solemn, her voice steady.

"You gave me freedom when I had none," she said. "You gave me a purpose beyond revenge. For that, I owe you my life."

Maximus met her gaze, his tone firm but kind. "You owe me nothing, Sheba. Your place among us is earned, not given."

Sheba knelt before him, her whip-sword resting across her palms. "Even so, I choose to follow you. I swear an oath to fight by your side, to protect this group, and to see your cause through to the end."

Han, Lee, Conan, and Ronan joined her, each placing a hand on their weapons as a sign of solidarity. Maximus, moved by their loyalty, placed his hand over theirs.

"Then let us fight as one," he said. "For honor, for justice, and for each other."

*A New Beginning*

From that day forward, Sheba became an integral part of Maximus's mighty men. Her past, though painful, no longer defined her. She fought not just for herself but for the group that had become her family. Together, they faced battles and challenges that tested their strength and unity, each victory bringing them closer to redemption.

Though she still carried the scars of her past, Sheba found solace in the bond she shared with her companions. With them, she was no longer a fallen princess or a gladiator—she was a warrior, a leader, and a friend.

# THE BARBARIAN HORDE AND
# THE RED GUARDIAN

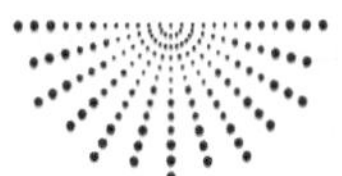

The journey to the Barbarian Falls was filled with trepidation. Known for its breathtaking beauty, the region was also home to a formidable barbarian tribe whose reputation for strength and tenacity was legendary, the Northern Barbarians. These are very wild beings, known for eating their dead and also their enemies. The group had heard the stories—towering figures, skilled in combat, and deeply rooted in traditions of honor and challenge. To cross through their territory was a calculated risk, but it was the only way to reach the falls and their ultimate goal.

The barbarian warriors were as imposing as the tales described: their towering stature, muscular builds, and commanding presence made them seem larger than life. Their skin bore the marks of their stories—ritual tattoos, battle scars, and decorative patterns carved with precision. They wore garments made from animal hides adorned with beads and bones, reflecting their connection to the land and their heritage. Every detail of their appearance spoke of strength, resilience, and an unyielding spirit.

Maximus led the group cautiously to the edge of the barbarian territory. "These people respect strength and directness," he said. "But they're also fiercely protective of their land. We must tread carefully."

Sheba, Lee, Ronan, and Nameless volunteered to accompany Maximus to meet the barbarian leader. Conan wanted to join the group, being a barbarian's king should hold some weight and possibly grant an easy passage... Maximus thought otherwise and left him behind and in charge. Di Vinci, despite Maximus's hesitations, insisted on joining them. "If we're not back by midday," Di Vinci said to Conan, "lead the others with caution. Avoid unnecessary conflict."

The group proceeded into the heart of barbarian territory, leaving their horses behind when the terrain became too rugged. The sound of waterfalls grew louder, mingling with the rustle of leaves and the occasional distant bird call. It was peaceful, but that peace was deceptive.

Without warning, a group of barbarians emerged from the dense foliage, their approach silent and coordinated. They moved with precision, encircling the group and signaling for them to stop. The barbarians' commander stepped forward—a towering figure with intricately braided hair and eyes that gleamed with intelligence. He gestured for the group to lower their weapons, his expression calm but firm.

Maximus raised his hands in a gesture of surrender.

"We come in peace," he said, his tone measured. "We seek an audience with your leader."

The barbarians exchanged glances before nodding. They gestured for the group to follow, their movements efficient and disciplined. The path led them through winding trails and rocky inclines until they reached the heart of the barbarian settlement. It was an impressive sight: structures built from natural materials blended seamlessly with the landscape, and the air buzzed with the energy of a tightly knit community.

The group was brought before Lodega, the barbarian leader. He stood out even among his people, his commanding presence and calm authority evident. His attire, crafted from fine hides and adorned with ceremonial patterns, spoke of his status. Around his neck hung a necklace of polished stones, each one glowing faintly in the sunlight

*The Trial of the Barbarians*

The group was dragged into the heart of the barbarian encampment, their captors moving with precise discipline. The settlement was both crude and imposing, with towering wooden barricades, massive stone structures, and smoke rising from multiple fires where the barbarians prepared their meals.

They were brought before Lodega, the supreme ruler of the barbarian tribe. "Lodega towered above the crowd, his coal-black skin gleaming in the firelight. His fur cloak and bone necklaces marked him as a conqueror, each trophy a story of triumph. His piercing eyes scanned the group, sharp and calculating."

Lodega's deep, booming voice echoed through the camp as he surveyed his captives. "The gods have truly favored me to bring the great General Maximus to my domain, along with his toy friends."

Maximus, standing as tall as he could despite his injuries, replied, "It is nice to see you too, Lodega."

Before he could finish, one of the barbarians struck him hard across the back, forcing him to drop to one knee.

"You infidel!" roared Gisha, a large barbarian with intricate scars running down his arms. "You only address him as the Supreme Ruler, or you die!"

Di Vinci stepped forward, his face filled with defiance. "Leave him be! Can't you see he's wounded?"

Gisha's hand came down hard, striking Di Vinci across the face and sending him sprawling to the ground. "You only speak when spoken to," Gisha growled.

Sheba stepped in to prevent Di Vinci from being singled out for interrogation. She claimed he was essential to their mission and took a hit meant for him.

Gisha raised his hand to hit him again, but Sheba didn't allow it. "Touch him again, and I'll kill you." her eyes were brimming with rage. Gisha chuckled and walked away.

Di Vinci: "You didn't have to do that."

Sheba: "Don't make me regret it."


*Lodega's Demand*

Lodega took a step closer, his massive frame casting a

shadow over the captives. His sharp eyes focused on Maximus. "Where is the barbarian ruler who abandoned his throne to follow a mere Roland slave? I don't see him anywhere. Is he dead or among the living?"

Maximus met his gaze, his tone steady. "We're only here to cross the falls. Let us pass, and we promise not to trouble you or your people."

Lodega's grin widened, his teeth gleaming. "Let you pass? Why would I do that when you would make such fine entertainment? By this afternoon, you'll grace the belly of our stew pot."

The barbarians laughed as Lodega's words echoed through the camp.

Lodega's tone grew more menacing. "The new god of the barbarians demands a strange man traveling among you. Who is he? Bring him forward."

"We don't know who you're talking about," Maximus said firmly.

"Liar," Lodega snapped. "If you're not here for the breeder's nest, then why come to my falls?" He turned to Gisha. "Send word to the god. Tell him we believe his quarry is among these fools."

Gisha stepped forward, pulling Di Vinci and Nameless roughly from the group. He loomed over them, his voice dripping with contempt. "Which one of you is he that the god seeks? Speak now, or both of you will suffer."

Neither answered.

Gisha sneered, drawing a dagger from his belt. Without hesitation, he stabbed Nameless in the shoulder and then Di Vinci, watching closely for any sign of unnatural healing. Both bled freely, showing no signs of recovery.

Disgusted, Gisha stormed back to Lodega. "Nothing," he spat.

*Nameless's Oath*

As the barbarians prepared for their feast, Maximus turned to Nameless; concern etched on his face. "Why didn't you heal?"

Nameless, his voice calm, replied, "I controlled the process. I'm fine."

Sheba, bound nearby, glared at him. "Good, because we need you to tear this place apart and leave nothing standing."

Nameless shook his head. "I can't do that."

Sheba's frustration boiled over. "What do you mean you can't? Can't you see we're about to be fed on?"

Maximus intervened. "Why not, Nameless? What's holding you back?"

Nameless lowered his gaze. "My oath as a Guardian. It forbids me from harming humans."

Maximus leaned closer, his voice firm. "If you don't act, we'll all die. And there will be no one left to name you."

Nameless sighed. "We're only tied because we allow it." With that, he stood, effortlessly breaking his restraints.

*The Duel*

The barbarians reacted instantly, rushing toward Nameless. But with fluid movements, he tossed them aside, his strength and precision unmatched. He approached Lodega, his voice steady. "I am the one you seek. But I offer a deal."

Lodega raised an eyebrow, intrigued. "A deal?"

"Fight Maximus," Nameless proposed. "If you win, you can take me and do what you will with the rest. If you lose, you let us pass."

Lodega laughed, the sound echoing through the camp. "You wish to settle this with a duel? Very well. I've been waiting to repay Maximus for the death of my brother."

Maximus's eyes widened in disbelief. "Are you insane? I can't fight him like this. My leg is broken!"

Nameless placed a hand on Maximus's shoulder. "Your body is programmed to heal itself. Trust me."

As Lodega removed his robes, his sheer size became evident. His body was a mass of muscles, his abdomen chiseled like stone, his biceps rippling with every movement. He stood over seven feet tall, his coal-black skin glistening in the firelight.

The duel began, and from the outset, Maximus was on the defensive. Lodega's strikes were powerful and relentless, each one forcing Maximus back. He fought valiantly, but it was clear he was outmatched.

Nameless knelt beside Maximus during a brief reprieve. "Only you can end this," he said. "You're underusing your mind. Ask me to help you."

Maximus nodded. "Help me."

Nameless guided him, instructing him to close his eyes and focus. As Lodega advanced for the final blow, Nameless's calm voice directed Maximus's movements. "Step right. Duck. Now strike."

Following Nameless's guidance, Maximus dodged Lodega's attacks with precision, each movement flowing seamlessly into the next. With each command, Maximus grew more confident, his strikes landing with greater force.

Finally, Maximus delivered a powerful blow that sent Lodega crashing to the ground. The barbarian leader lay motionless, defeated.

*The Aftermath*

Nameless stepped forward, his voice steady. "We won. Let us pass. That was the deal."

As Lodega lay there, Gisha approached, offering his hand to help the king rise. Instead, he slit Lodega's throat, held him firmly until his body was lifeless. "There is no deal," Gisha snarled.

The barbarians roared, drawing their weapons. But before they could attack, an arrow landed at Gisha's feet.

Conan, the priest, Han, and Lugo stood atop a ridge, their weapons drawn. "That was a warning shot," the priest called. "The next one will be between your eyes."

Conan's voice boomed. "I am Conan, king of the barbarians of the west and south. Defy me, and you will all fall."

Enraged, Gisha roared, "Kill them!"

The camp descended into chaos as the battle began.

. . .

## The Clash at the Barbarian Camp

The camp erupted into chaos at Gisha's command. The barbarians surged forward, their roars blending with the clang of steel as they charged the group. Conan, Han, Lugo, and the priest leapt down from the ridge, joining the fray with unparalleled precision and determination.

## The Battle Begins

Conan met the first wave of attackers head-on, his massive blade carving a path through the horde. "Barbarians of the west and south do not fall to traitors!" he bellowed, his voice cutting through the din of battle. His strikes were swift and devastating, each one landing with precision.

Lugo, his axe gleaming in the firelight, fought beside Conan. The two were an unrelenting force, their weapons creating a deadly rhythm. "These fools don't know who they're dealing with," Lugo growled, swinging his axe in a wide arc that forced several barbarians back.

Han and Lee moved together like shadows, their acrobatic flips and fluid strikes keeping their enemies off balance. Han's twin blades danced in the air, cutting through any who dared approach, while Lee used his speed to land devastating blows at critical points.

The priest, perched on higher ground, fired arrow after arrow into the fray. Each shot was precise, finding its mark with unerring accuracy. His voice rang out with calm orders, coordinating their movements amidst the chaos.

## Nameless and the Gremors

Nameless stood at the center, his focus shifting between the attacking barbarians and the Gremors looming in the distance. He could sense the shifting tide, the creeping danger that neither side yet realized. "They're coming," he muttered to himself, his grip tightening on his swords.

The Gremors, led by the Red Guardian, began to move. Their hulking forms descended into the camp, their claws tearing through the remaining barbarian defenses with terrifying ease.

## Barbarians vs. Gremors

The barbarians turned as the first of the Gremors struck. One creature, larger than any they had faced, barreled through a group of warriors, its claws slashing in wide, deadly arcs. The once-organized ranks of the barbarians dissolved into panic as the Gremors began their onslaught.

Gisha shouted orders, rallying his men to fight the creatures. "Hold the line! They're nothing more than beasts!" he roared, but his voice was drowned out by the shrieks and roars of the Gremors.

Lodega's loyalists, caught between their retreat and the advancing Gremors, were quickly overwhelmed. The beasts showed no mercy, tearing through anyone in their path.

.   .   .

*The Group's Fight Against the Gremors*

As the barbarians fell, the group turned their attention to the Gremors. Maximus shouted, "Stay together! These creatures are more dangerous than anything we've faced before!"

Nameless charged into the fray, his swords flashing as he engaged one of the beasts. His movements were a blur, each strike aimed with deadly precision. He shouted back to the others, "Focus on their weak points—the joints and underbelly!"

Conan and Lugo fought side by side, their combined strength forcing a Gremor back. "You take the legs; I'll take the head!" Conan called, slashing at the creature's flank as Lugo brought his axe down on its knee, crippling it.

Sheba and Lee flanked another Gremor, using their agility to evade its strikes and land coordinated blows. Lee slid beneath the creature, slicing at its exposed underbelly, while Sheba leapt onto its back, driving her blade into its spine.

The priest, from his vantage point, loosed a volley of arrows at the advancing creatures, each shot carefully aimed at their glowing eyes. One by one, his arrows found their marks, momentarily blinding the beasts and giving his allies an opening to strike.


*The Arrival of the Red Guardian*

Amidst the chaos, the Red Guardian stood atop a large Gremor, his presence commanding. His crimson armor seemed to pulse with life, and his gaze swept across the battlefield with cold indifference. He raised a hand, and the Gremors halted their attack, turning their attention toward him.

The remaining barbarians, battered and bloodied, turned as well, their fear giving way to confusion. "What is he?" one whispered, his voice trembling.

Nameless stepped forward, his voice steady despite the terror in his eyes. "He's the one who took my name. The Red Guardian."

The Guardian's gaze settled on Nameless. "You've caused me quite the inconvenience," he said, his voice calm but menacing. "But no more games. Surrender now, and I might spare your friends."

Nameless tightened his grip on his swords. "I won't let you hurt them."

The Guardian tilted his head, a faint smirk on his lips. "You can't even save yourself."

*Gremors Turn on the Barbarians*

With a flick of the Guardian's wrist, the Gremors surged forward once more—but this time, their targets were indiscriminate. Barbarians who had moments ago been their allies now found themselves under attack. The creatures tore through the camp, their ferocity unmatched

Gisha, refusing to flee, rallied the remaining warriors. "We are barbarians! We don't run from beasts!" he shouted, charging at one of the Gremors. He landed a powerful blow with his axe, but the creature retaliated, its claws tearing through his defenses.

The camp became a slaughter as the Gremors overwhelmed both the barbarians and their defenses.

*The Group's Stand Against the Red Guardian*

The group regrouped, their focus shifting to the Red Guardian. Maximus turned to the others. "If we don't stop him here, no one will."

Nameless, his voice steady but grim, replied, "You don't understand. He's a Guardian. Even if we fight together, we can't match his power."

Maximus set his jaw. "Then we make our own rules."

The group charged together, their movements coordinated. Conan and Lugo attacked from the front, their weapons striking in unison, while Sheba and Lee flanked from either side. Nameless moved with precision, his strikes aimed at exploiting any openings.

The Red Guardian met their assault with ease, parrying each blow with almost casual movements. His crimson blade flashed in the firelight, its every swing forcing the group back.

"You're persistent," he said, his tone mocking. "But persistence is not strength."

*Nameless's Resolve*

As the group faltered, Nameless stepped forward, his determination unwavering. "You've taken everything from me," he said, his voice filled with quiet fury. "It ends here."

The Red Guardian smirked. "You think you can stop me? You couldn't even protect your name."

# THE FLIGHT THROUGH THE WOODS

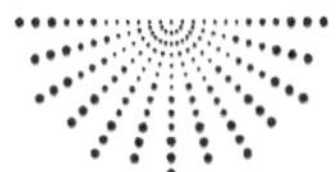

The Red Guardian stood tall, his crimson armor glowing faintly as he addressed the group. "Give me the Nameless One, and I might just let you all live. You've come so far in trying to stop me; I will show mercy, for I am a god among your kind."

Ronan sneered, his grip tightening on his blade. "Did you hear that?" he asked, turning to the others.

Sheba smirked. "I heard it, but it sounds like a child crying for attention."

Lugo added with a shrug, "I heard nothing, only the wind."

The Guardian's calm demeanor faltered, a flicker of irritation crossing his face. With a swift gesture, he unleashed the Gremors. "You dare mock me? Face your doom."

## The Battle Against the Gremors

The Gremors moved like shadows, their speed and agility rivaling the legendary Protectors. Nameless, consumed by a fiery anger, met them head-on. His swords flashed in the firelight as he tore through the creatures with relentless precision.

The others fought valiantly alongside him. Maximus and Conan struck with deadly efficiency, their blades finding the creatures' weak points. Lugo and Ronan fought back-to-back, their strikes keeping the beasts at bay. Sheba and Lee used their agility to dart between the Gremors, landing critical blows before retreating to safety.

Amidst the chaos, Han and Lee saw an opportunity to strike at the Red Guardian directly. With a series of acrobatic flips, they closed the distance, their blades aimed at the Guardian's exposed sides.

Nameless saw their approach and screamed, "No!!!"

But it was too late. In a single, fluid motion, the Guardian moved, his crimson blade slicing through the air. Han and Lee's bodies fell lifeless to the ground, their attack ended before it could begin.

## The Red Guardian's Power

The priest, horrified, loosed a volley of arrows at the Guardian. Each arrow froze mid-air as the Guardian raised a hand, stopping them with his mind. Slowly, the arrows turned, pointing back toward their source.

"Futile," the Guardian said, his voice cold. With a flick of his wrist, the arrows shot forward, striking the priest through his chest and limbs. He fell, his bow slipping from his grasp.

Nameless, watching the carnage, gritted his teeth and focused. Using his mind, he pulled the arrows from the priest's body and hurled them at the Guardian. The Guardian stopped them effortlessly, reversing their trajectory once more.

Nameless tried to dodge, but the speed was too great. One arrow pierced his side, lodging deep in his ribcage. He broke off the shaft, his breathing ragged, and charged at the Guardian.

The two clashed, their blades meeting in a shower of sparks. Nameless fought with all his strength, but the Guardian's power was overwhelming. Each strike pushed Nameless further back, his wounds multiplying as the Guardian's blade appeared and disappeared with uncanny speed.

Finally, the Guardian drove Nameless to the ground, blood pooling beneath him. He raised his blade for the final strike, his eyes cold and merciless.

*A Desperate Escape*

Before the blow could land, Maximus leapt forward, tackling the Guardian with all his strength. The impact knocked the Guardian back momentarily. As he rose, Lugo charged in, wrapping his massive arms around the Guardian's torso in a crushing vice grip.

"Run!" Lugo shouted to Maximus and Conan. "Take him and go!"

Lugo(gritting his teeth): "Go, Maximus! Protect Rome!"

Maximus (shouting): "No! I won't leave you!"

Lugo: "This is my glory. Tell Rome I died a giant, and better not forget me."

"I'll remember you," Said Maximus in a whisper.

Maximus and Conan lifted Nameless and ran toward the woods. Behind them, Lugo held the Guardian with all his might.

The Guardian's voice rang out, low and ominous. "You cannot escape me, foolish humans." With a surge of strength, he ripped Lugo's arms from his body. Lugo's scream echoed through the camp before the Guardian silenced him with a swift strike.

Ronan charged at the Guardian, only to be met with the same fate. The Guardian's blade swung in a deadly arc, and Ronan's head fell to the ground. Sheba, attempting to intervene, was struck down, her body crumpling unconscious.

The Guardian turned, his voice calm and commanding. "Gremors, find them. Bring them to me."


*The Chase Through the Woods*

Maximus and Conan ran through the dense forest, carrying the injured Nameless between them. The sound of snapping branches and guttural growls grew louder as the Gremors closed in.

"They're coming!" Conan hissed, his eyes scanning the darkness.

Maximus gritted his teeth. "We need to lose them."

They twisted and turned through the woods, but the creatures followed _relentlessly. Finally, Conan stopped, placing Nameless against a tree.

The forest was a labyrinth of towering trees and tangled undergrowth, the air thick with the scent of earth and damp leaves. Maximus and Conan pushed forward, carrying Nameless between them. Nameless's body was limp, his breathing labored, blood soaking through his clothes. Behind them, the guttural growls of the Gremors grew louder, their heavy footfalls shaking the ground.

"They're gaining on us," Conan muttered, his voice tight with urgency. "We won't outrun them like this."

Maximus gritted his teeth, his muscles straining under Nameless's weight. "We don't have a choice. We have to try."

The moonlight barely pierced through the dense canopy above, casting the forest in shadows. The sound of snapping branches and the guttural snarls of the Gremors echoed ominously. The beasts were closing in, their predatory instincts guiding them unerringly through the maze of trees.

*A Plan of Sacrifice*

Conan suddenly stopped, setting Nameless gently against the trunk of a large oak tree. "This isn't going to work," he said firmly. "You need to get him to safety. I'll hold them off."

Maximus turned to his friend, his expression a mix of defiance and sorrow. "No. We do this together."

Conan shook his head. "You know as well as I do that he's our only chance against that monster. If we both stay here, none of us makes it out alive."

Maximus hesitated, his grip tightening on Nameless's arm. "To death and glory, my friend."

Conan smiled faintly. "And all the way to the afterlife, my brother. Now go!"


## *The Gremors Arrive*

Maximus hoisted Nameless onto his back and resumed running. Conan drew his sword, the metal gleaming faintly in the dim light. He climbed a nearby tree, positioning himself among its thick branches.

The first Gremor emerged from the shadows, its massive form moving with an unnatural grace. It sniffed the air, its glowing eyes scanning the forest floor. Two more followed close behind, their claws tearing at the ground as they moved.

Conan held his breath, waiting for the perfect moment. As the first Gremor passed beneath him, he leapt from the tree, driving his sword into the beast's skull. The creature let out a deafening screech, its body collapsing to the ground.

The other two Gremors turned toward the sound, their predatory instincts honing in on Conan. He pulled his sword free and readied himself, a fierce determination in his eyes.

· · ·

*The Pursuit Continues*

Farther ahead, Maximus pushed through the under-growth, his breath coming in heavy bursts. Nameless stirred weakly on his back.

"They're still coming," Nameless muttered, his voice barely audible.

Maximus glanced over his shoulder, his face grim. "Then we'll keep going."

Behind them, the distant scream of the fallen Gremor echoed through the forest. Maximus's heart clenched. He knew Conan was fighting bravely, but he also knew the odds were against him.

The sound of snapping branches and heavy footsteps drew closer. The remaining Gremors were relentless, their guttural growls growing louder with every passing second.

*The Cliff's Edge*

Maximus burst through a dense thicket, the sudden openness startling him. Before him was a sheer drop, the edge of a cliff overlooking a rushing river far below. The water shimmered faintly in the moonlight, its roar filling the air.

He set Nameless down carefully. The Guardian's brother was pale, his breaths shallow.

"You have to leave me," Nameless said weakly, his voice hoarse. "I can't make that jump. Save yourself."

Maximus knelt beside him, gripping his shoulder firmly. "Do you think my brothers died so that I could run and hide? No. They died so you could live. You are the only chance we have against your brother. Whether you like it or not, you're going to live, and we're going to find your name. We're going to stop him."

Nameless's eyes flickered with a faint glimmer of hope, but his body remained too weak to protest further.

The snapping of branches and growls of the Gremors broke the moment. The creatures had caught up, their massive forms emerging from the trees. Their glowing eyes locked onto the pair, and their claws dug into the earth as they prepared to lunge.

*The Leap of Faith*

Maximus stood, his hand tightening around Nameless's arm. "Hold on," he said, his voice steady.

As the Gremors charged, Maximus hoisted Nameless onto his back and sprinted toward the cliff's edge. The ground seemed to fall away beneath them as they leapt into the void.

The wind roared in their ears as they plummeted toward the river. The Gremors reached the edge moments later, their poor eyesight preventing them from spotting the duo in the water below. With guttural growls of frustration, they hesitated briefly before leaping after them.

*In the River*

The icy water enveloped Maximus and Nameless as they hit the river. The current was strong, pulling them downstream at a rapid pace. Maximus struggled to keep both of them afloat, his arms burning with effort.

The Gremors splashed into the river behind them, their massive forms barely hindered by the rushing water. Their guttural growls reverberated through the canyon as they resumed their pursuit.

Maximus glanced over his shoulder, his face set with grim determination. "I'm not losing you," he muttered, tightening his grip on Nameless as he swam toward the riverbank.

*A Momentary Escape*

Reaching the shore, Maximus dragged Nameless onto the muddy ground, both of them gasping for air. The Gremors, hindered by their bulk and the force of the current, struggled to climb out of the water.

Maximus helped Nameless to his feet, his voice firm. "We need to keep moving. They won't stay down for long."

Nameless nodded weakly, leaning heavily on Maximus as they disappeared into the forest.

Above them, on the edge of the cliff, the Red Guardian watched, his expression unreadable. "You cannot run forever," he said softly, his voice carrying through the night.

*Lugo...*

The Warlord of the North

Lugo was born in the icy wilderness of the far north, in

a small village that thrived against all odds amidst harsh winters and treacherous terrain. From an early age, he was recognized as exceptional—taller, stronger, and fiercer than any of his peers. By the time he was fifteen, he stood a head taller than the village's tallest warrior, his immense frame earning him the title "The Giant of Frostborn."

The people of his village valued strength above all else, and Lugo quickly rose to prominence. He became a leader in their battles against rival clans, his colossal axe carving through enemies like they were mere twigs. But Lugo was more than a warrior—he was a protector. He fought to defend his people, his family, and his way of life.

*The Loss of Frostborn*

When Lugo was twenty-five, his life took a devastating turn. During a particularly harsh winter, raiders descended upon Frostborn. These were not the usual warring clans but a horde led by a cruel and cunning warlord named Jorrik the Blight. Jorrik had no interest in honor or conquest—he sought only to destroy.

The battle was fierce, and Lugo fought valiantly, cutting down dozens of raiders with his mighty axe. But even his immense strength was not enough. The invaders overwhelmed Frostborn, setting the village ablaze and slaughtering its people.

By the time the sun rose, Lugo was the only survivor. He stood amidst the ruins of his home, his hands bloodied, his body battered, and his heart shattered. His wife and daughter, the lights of his life, were among the fallen. Their lifeless bodies lay in the snow, their once-vibrant faces frozen in fear.

Lugo fell to his knees, his grief transforming into a roar that echoed through the mountains. In that moment, he vowed that he would never allow such devastation to happen again. He swore to become a warrior so formidable that no force on earth could stand against him. But beneath his vow burned a deeper, darker desire—a longing for a worthy death, one that would give his pain meaning.

*The Wanderer*

For years, Lugo wandered the world, seeking purpose. He became a mercenary, selling his sword to the highest bidder. His reputation grew with each battle—his size and strength made him a living legend, and his axe became a symbol of unrelenting destruction.

But as the years passed, Lugo found little satisfaction in his victories. The battles were meaningless, the causes unworthy. He began to crave something greater—an adventure that would test his limits, a cause that would justify the blood he shed.

One fateful day, while journeying through the dense forests of Germania, Lugo encountered a group of bandits attacking a caravan. He watched from the shadows as a small band of warriors fought valiantly against overwhelming odds. Among them was a man who stood out—not for his size or ferocity, but for his leadership and unwavering determination. It was Maximus.

. . .

*A Fateful Encounter*

Lugo watched as Maximus and his companions—Han, Lee, Conan, and Sheba—fought with skill and precision. The bandits fell one by one, but their numbers were too great. For the first time in years, Lugo felt a flicker of purpose. He hefted his axe and charged into the fray.

The sight of Lugo—a towering giant wielding a massive axe—sent the bandits into a panic. He cut through them like a force of nature, his every swing leaving destruction in its wake. Within moments, the battle was over.

Maximus approached Lugo, his expression a mix of gratitude and curiosity. "You fight with the strength of a hundred men," he said. "What brings you to this forest?"

Lugo, his voice deep and resonant, replied simply, "I seek purpose."

Maximus studied him for a moment before nodding. "Then perhaps you've found it."

*Earning His Place*

At first, Lugo was an outsider among Maximus's group. His size and stoic demeanor made him intimidating, and his blunt nature often clashed with the more refined personalities of Han and Lee. Conan, however, saw a kindred spirit in Lugo and quickly bonded with him over their shared love of battle.

Lugo's true test came during a mission to liberate a

village from a tyrannical warlord. The group was ambushed, and Maximus was gravely injured. With the odds stacked against them, Lugo took charge, rallying the others and leading a counterattack. His strength and courage turned the tide of the battle, and the warlord was defeated.

After the victory, Maximus, still recovering, approached Lugo. "You could have left us," he said. "But you stayed. Why?"

Lugo looked at him, his gaze steady. "Because you fight for something real. Something worth dying for."

Maximus extended his hand. "Then fight with us. Not as a mercenary, but as a brother."

Lugo took his hand, his grip firm. "I swear it. To the end."

*The Oath*

That night, around a roaring fire, Lugo swore an oath to Maximus and the group. "I have wandered too long, seeking a death worthy of my strength. But now, I see that life can be just as worthy. I will fight for you, Maximus. For your cause. And when the day comes that I fall, I will fall with honor, knowing I stood with the greatest warriors I have ever known."

Han and Lee, who had initially been wary of Lugo, raised their weapons in solidarity. Conan clapped him on the back, grinning. Sheba, ever the pragmatist, simply nodded. Maximus placed a hand on Lugo's shoulder, his voice steady. "Then let us fight as one."

.  .  .

*A Giant with a Purpose*

From that day forward, Lugo became an indispensable member of Maximus's mighty men. His strength and courage inspired those around him, and his bond with the group grew stronger with each battle.

Though he still carried the pain of his past, Lugo found solace in the camaraderie of his newfound family. And while he no longer sought death, he remained ready to face it—on his own terms and for a cause greater than himself.

# 8

# THE ORB AND THE CALL FOR REINFORCEMENTS

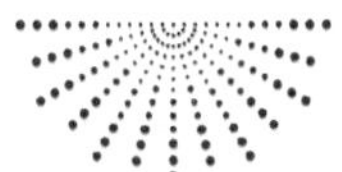

The roaring current swept Maximus and Nameless through the river's unforgiving course. Water surged around them, tossing them like leaves in a storm. Rocks scraped their sides, and debris tangled in their limbs, but Maximus held onto Nameless with all his strength. The river's roar grew louder, and before Maximus could process what was happening, they were hurled off the edge of a massive waterfall.

They plummeted into the misty abyss, the icy water crashing over them with bone-jarring force. When they resurfaced, gasping for air, the river's flow finally slowed, depositing them onto a rocky bank. Exhausted and battered, Maximus dragged Nameless ashore.

As Maximus took in his surroundings, his eyes widened. The waterfall behind them was the very one they had been searching for. It cascaded down a jagged cliffside, its base concealed by mist and shadow. Despite his aching body, a flicker of hope ignited within him.

But that hope was short-lived. Nameless's condition had worsened. His body was covered in wet, festering sores, and the stench of decay was unbearable.

*Nameless's Deterioration*

Maximus carried Nameless to a secluded spot under the cover of dense foliage. He set him down gently, shielding him from the open. It was a hole in the rock that led to nowhere. Both men were exhausted, as for Maximus, he needed to catch his breath. After a long silence, lying in the dark, he broke the silence. Sitting beside the glowing of the moon. Nameless's condition was deteriorating.

Maximus: "This name of yours (he spoke quietly)… why does it matter so much?"

Nameless looked into the light of the moon and said: "A Guardian's name is more than a word. It's our essence, our power. Without it, I'm incomplete—a shadow of myself."

Maximus: "And Shamanu stole yours?"

Nameless (nodding weakly): "He broke the law of the Guardians, using forbidden power to sever it from me. My name is locked in this orb, waiting to be reclaimed."

"You stay here," Maximus said, his voice firm but desperate. "Focus on healing while I scout the area."

Nameless barely opened his eyes, his voice a weak whisper. "I can't… It's too late…"

Don't you dare give up," Maximus snapped, determination overriding his fear.

With nothing but two knives for protection, Maximus ventured cautiously into the surrounding area. The forest was eerily silent except for the thunderous roar of another waterfall in the distance. He crept closer, weaving through dense trees and overgrown brush, until he reached a clearing.

What he saw made his blood run cold.

Over a dozen Gremors lay sprawled in the shallow waters, their massive forms writhing as if in restless slumber. Unbeknownst to Maximus, he had taken cover behind the Breeder herself. The creature's gargantuan form loomed like a nightmare, her body grotesquely swollen and rippling with unnatural muscle. She was as tall as a tree, her limbs as wide as a valley, and her many eyes glistened faintly in the mist.

Behind her, partially hidden by the waterfall's cascading sheets of water, Maximus spotted a dark opening—a cave.

He retreated carefully, his heart pounding in his chest. The Breeder stirred slightly, her massive head tilting as if sensing his presence. Maximus held his breath until he was far enough to move quickly back toward Nameless.


*The Orb of Shuwannu*

Returning to Nameless, Maximus found him in a horrifying state. His body was deteriorating rapidly, his skin darkening and sloughing off in places. The smell of rot was overwhelming.

"What's happening to you? Why aren't you healing?" Maximus demanded, panic in his voice.

Nameless opened his eyes weakly. "The Red Guardian… poisoned me. I can't heal. I'm… dying."

"No," Maximus said firmly, crouching beside him. "You're not dying. Not on my watch. I've found the cave where your name is."

Nameless tried to shake his head. "There's… no time… Just let me go…"

Maximus lifted him into his arms, ignoring the stench and the feeble protests. "Shut up. How will I know your name when I see it?"

"You'll… know," Nameless rasped, his voice barely audible. "Don't… worry about that."

Carrying Nameless through the forest, Maximus slipped past the Breeder and into the cave. The air inside was cool and heavy, the faint glow of an otherworldly light drawing him deeper.

At the center of the cave sat the orb, resting atop a jagged rock. It was a perfect sphere, shimmering with liquid energy that defied gravity. The orb seemed alive, its surface rippling faintly as if responding to his presence.

Maximus laid Nameless on the ground near the orb. "I found it," he said, his voice trembling with urgency. "I found your name. What do I do with this thing? How does it work?"

Nameless, his body now almost lifeless, whispered, "The orb… It will tell you…"

Maximus picked up the orb, its surface warm and vibrating faintly. "Alright, tell me your name so I can name you," he said, his frustration mounting.

Nameless managed a faint smile. "You're so… stupid. Let the orb… tell you…", weakly, but with a faint smirk he added, "You'll hear it, Maximus... The orb speaks to those who listen."

With that, his chest rose and fell one last time. His body stilled, and the light faded from his eyes.

"No!" Maximus shouted, shaking him. "Stay with me! Nameless, wake up!"

The sound of guttural growls echoed from the cave entrance. The stench of decay had drawn the Gremors, and their massive forms began to fill the space.

Tears streamed down Maximus's face as he raised the orb above his head, its light intensifying as his emotions poured into it. "I name you Shuwannu!" he cried, his voice echoing through the cavern. He placed the orb on Nameless's chest, but nothing happened.

*Rome Prepares for War*

Far away, in the heart of Rome, the Senate was alive with fervent debate. Word had arrived from General Marcus, carried by a messenger who bore the claw of a Gremor as grim evidence of the threat they faced.

The messenger's account painted a dire picture: Maximus and his forces were deep in barbarian territory, facing unimaginable horrors. Marcus's plea for reinforcements echoed in the Senate chambers, where senators argued over the best course of action.

Senator Aralus, a man known for his ambition and cunning, seized the moment. "This is our opportunity to showcase the might of Rome," he declared, his voice resonating with authority. "Let us march to their aid—not as mere reinforcements, but as saviors. Let the people see that Rome does not falter, even in the face of monsters!"

The chamber buzzed with murmurs of agreement. Aralus's allies quickly rallied behind him, their support bolstered by promises of glory and political leverage.

When word reached Caesar, he listened carefully to Aralus's impassioned plea. "Maximus is a capable general," Caesar said thoughtfully. "Should we not trust his judgment and send aid as he requested?"

Aralus bowed deeply, his tone reverent but persuasive. "Your Majesty, Maximus's valor is unquestionable. But this is no ordinary battle. Allow me to lead the cavalry and ensure Rome's triumph. Let the people see the strength of their Senate and their emperor."

After a moment's hesitation, Caesar nodded. "Very well. You shall lead the reinforcements. But remember, Aralus—failure is not an option."

As preparations began, Aralus stood in the Senate's grand hall, a self-satisfied smile on his face. Rome was mobilizing, but the battle ahead was one that neither he nor the soldiers marching with him could fully comprehend.

*The Priest...*

The Forest Outlaw

Born in the rugged wilderness of Britannia, Kaelus grew up in a land ruled by tyranny and oppression. His village, nestled deep in the ancient forests, was constantly under threat from Roman overlords and local warlords, who taxed the peasants into destitution. The people lived in fear, their lives bound by the whims of the powerful.

Kaelus's father, a woodsman, taught him the ways of the forest—how to move silently, track prey, and wield a bow with deadly precision. These lessons were not just for survival; they became a means of rebellion. By the time Kaelus was seventeen, he had turned his skills into a weapon against oppression, stealing from the overlords and redistributing the wealth to the starving villagers.

The people of Britannia began to whisper his name with awe and gratitude, calling him the Hooded Archer, a symbol of hope in dark times. But the overlords viewed him as a threat and put a bounty on his head. For years, Kaelus evaded capture, his knowledge of the forests making him a ghost among the trees.

*The Archer and the Cross*

Kaelus's exploits made him a folk hero, but they also painted a target on his back. One fateful day, his luck ran out. Betrayed by someone he had trusted, Kaelus was captured by Roman soldiers. He was brought before the local Roman governor, a man known for his cruelty and love of public executions.

Sentenced to death by crucifixion, Kaelus was paraded through the streets of the Roman garrison. Stripped of his hood and bound in chains, he was mocked and jeered by the same people he had sought to help. The betrayal and ingratitude cut deeper than the physical wounds he had sustained during his capture. But Kaelus's story did not end there.

*The Arrival of Maximus*

On the day of Kaelus's execution, a Roman general, Maximus, passed through the garrison on his way to the northern front. Maximus was intrigued by the stories of the Hooded Archer and requested an audience with the condemned man.

In their meeting, Maximus saw not a criminal but a man of conviction—a rebel who fought not for personal gain but for the weak and downtrodden. He admired Kaelus's spirit, even if he did not condone his methods.

"What drives a man to risk his life for others?" Maximus asked.

Kaelus, his voice hoarse from days without water, replied, "If I don't, who will? The people cry out for justice, but the gods remain silent. Someone has to act."

Impressed by Kaelus's courage and determination, Maximus offered him a choice: execution or redemption. "Join me," Maximus said. "Fight for something greater than vengeance. Prove to the world that justice can be achieved without bloodlust."

*A Thief's Redemption*

Kaelus accepted the offer, though he remained wary of Maximus's intentions. Freed from his chains, he accompanied the general and his legion to the northern front. At first, the soldiers distrusted him, viewing him as little more than a common thief. But Kaelus quickly proved his worth.

During an ambush by barbarian raiders, Kaelus's unmatched skill with a bow turned the tide of battle. His arrows flew thru, taking down enemies before they could reach the Roman lines. The soldiers began to respect him, and Maximus saw in Kaelus the potential for greatness.

Over time, Kaelus shed his identity as the Hooded Archer and embraced a new path. He began to study philosophy and faith, seeking to atone for the lives he had taken and the pain he had caused. His sharp wit and newfound wisdom earned him the nickname "The Priest" among his comrades.

*Joining the Mighty Men*

When Maximus formed his elite team, Kaelus was among the first to be chosen. By this time, he had fully embraced his new identity, fighting not for personal gain but for the greater good. His golden bow—a gift from Maximus—became a symbol of his transformation, a weapon of protection rather than theft.

Kaelus quickly bonded with the other members of the team. Han and Lee admired his precision and often trained with him in secret competitions. Conan respected his sharp mind and began to see him as a brother in arms. Even Sheba, known for her sharp tongue and distrust of others, came to value The Priest's calm demeanor and unshakable faith.

*The Archer's Faith*

Though Kaelus no longer identified as a thief, he retained his rebellious spirit. He believed in fighting for the oppressed and saw Maximus's mission as an extension of his own. His faith—born of hardship and redemption—became a guiding light for the team, offering hope in their darkest moments.

To this day, The Priest carries his golden bow, a reminder of the life he left behind and the path he now walks. He remains a quiet, steady presence among Maximus's mighty men, his arrows always ready to defend the innocent and strike down those who prey on the weak.

*Legacy*

In the forests of Britannia, the legend of the Hooded Archer lives on. Though the man himself has left, his deeds inspire others to rise against tyranny and fight for justice, like Robin Hood of Loxley. And though Kaelus is now The Priest, he carries the spirit of the Hooded Archer wherever he goes, a silent protector and a beacon of hope.

# 9

# THE RETURN OF THE BLUE GUARDIAN

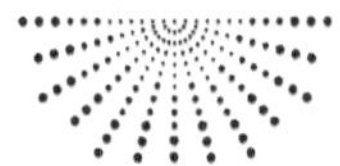

The cave was still, save for the faint hum of the orb now resting inside Nameless's chest. Maximus stood over his fallen companion, tears streaking his bloodstained face. The sound of guttural growls grew louder as the Gremors closed in, drawn by the stench of death.

Wiping his eyes, Maximus rose, gripping his knives tightly. The first Gremors entered the cave, their massive forms blocking the entrance. The creatures jostled and snarled, each eager to claim their prey. The largest among them stepped forward, towering over the others, its glowing eyes fixed on Maximus.

Maximus stepped forward, trembling with both fear and rage. "Let's finish this," he muttered, gripping his knives.

The Gremor roared, shaking the walls of the cave, and Maximus charged. Before he could strike, a blinding blue light erupted from behind him. The Gremors froze, their howls replaced by shrieks of pain as they began to explode, their bodies bursting into chunks of flesh and bone.

Maximus shielded his eyes as the cave filled with blue flames. When he looked up, the Gremors were gone, and standing before him was Shuwannu—the Blue Guardian. He hovered a foot above the ground, his armor glowing with ethereal energy.

Shuwannu stepped forward, his expression calm but resolute. "You are General Maximus, the Brave. Your sacrifices have not gone unnoticed. You and your companions fought valiantly to bring me here. I am in your debt."

Maximus, still stunned, managed to stammer, "You... know me? We fought side by side once."

Shuwannu nodded. "Indeed. And now I fight for your world. Stay here. There is a Breeder outside. I will handle her."

Shuwannu turned toward the cave's exit.

"It's Gremor, not Kiballangu," Maximus called out, confused by the Guardian's terminology.

"What?" Shuwannu asked, tilting his head.

"Never mind," Maximus muttered.


*The Breeder's Wrath*

As Shuwannu approached the exit, the Breeder struck the rocks, attempting to seal them inside. Her massive body loomed outside, surrounded by her offspring, who leaped and snarled in anticipation.

Suddenly, a blast of blue flames shattered the debris, sending shards flying. Shuwannu leaped out of the cave, carrying Maximus with him, and deposited the general on the mountaintop.

"This won't take long," Shuwannu said, turning to face the colossal Breeder. "Stay safe."

The Breeder roared, her voice shaking the earth, as Shuwannu charged. The battle was fierce and relentless. The Guardian, though only six feet tall, moved with lightning speed and precision, his strikes cutting deep into the monstrous creature.

The Breeder retaliated, swiping with claws as large as trees, but Shuwannu dodged effortlessly. Her offspring joined the fray, forcing him to divide his attention. Blue flames erupted from his hands, reducing the smaller Gremors to ash as he focused his assault on the Breeder.

*Maximus and Conan's Fight*

As Maximus watched the epic battle below, two Gremors crept up behind him. He turned, drawing his knives, hoping to intimidate them. Instead, the creatures glanced at each other and let out mocking laughs.

"Seriously? You're laughing at me?" Maximus muttered, frustration boiling over.

Before the Gremors could strike, a massive sword pierced the knee of one. The creature collapsed with a shriek, and Conan stepped into view, his blade gleaming.

"Miss me?" Conan said with a grin, cutting down the fallen Gremor.

Maximus leaped onto the back of the second Gremor,

driving his knives into its hide. The beast thrashed wildly, but Maximus held firm until Conan severed its limbs.

As the creature fell, Maximus and Conan stood side by side, catching their breath. "Good to see you alive," Maximus said.

"Likewise," Conan replied. "But we've got no time to celebrate."

### The Breeder's End

Down below, Shuwannu delivered a devastating final blow, his energy blade piercing the Breeder's massive heart. The creature let out a final, earsplitting roar before collapsing. Her offspring scattered, leaderless and terrified.

Shuwannu stood amidst the carnage, washing the Breeder's blood from his hands in the river. Maximus and Conan approached cautiously.

"It's over," Maximus said, his voice filled with relief.

Shuwannu turned to them, his gaze somber. "No. It's not. The male is still out there, and Shamanu, the Red Guardian, won't stop until the eggs are hatched."

As he spoke, Shuwannu threw a boomerang blade into the woods. It sliced through the air, cutting down a tree. From the shadows, Di Vinci stumbled into view.

"Di Vinci!" Maximus exclaimed, stunned.

"I'm not that easy to kill," Di Vinci replied, grinning.

### The Final Army

Moments later, Di Vinci revealed that reinforcements

had arrived—a massive Roman army equipped with giant crossbows, catapults, and siege weapons. Senator Aralus had brought them, hoping to claim glory for himself.

The soldiers stood in formation, their faces pale with fear. Di Vinci turned to Maximus. "The men need you. Rally them. Behind us lie eggs that could doom us all. But ahead of us stands the strength of Rome. And if these monsters think we'll falter, they know nothing of who we are!"

Maximus rode to the front of the line, addressing the troops. "Men of Rome! If you run, I won't blame you. But know this: if these monsters break through, they will destroy everything—our homes, our families, our world.

The soldiers roared in response, their fear replaced by determination.


*Shuwannu vs. Shamanu*

As the Gremors surged forward, Shamanu and the male Breeder led the charge. Shuwannu met his brother in the middle of the battlefield.

"I see you've reclaimed your name," Shamanu sneered. "But you've always been weak."

"I am Shuwannu, the Blue Guardian of Alganu," Shuwannu replied. "You will face justice for your crimes."

Shamanu (mocking): "Your name was the first thing I took from you, brother. And now, I'll take your world."

Shuwannu: "My name is mine again. And with it, I'll end this."

Their battle was unlike anything seen before. The two

Guardians leaped across mountains, their strikes sending shockwaves through the battlefield.

### Aralus's Fall

Meanwhile, Senator Aralus, eager for glory, led a charge against the male Breeder. The creature swatted him aside effortlessly, crushing him beneath its massive claws.

Di Vinci and Maximus devised a daring plan to take down the beast. With Sheba tied to its neck like a pendant, Maximus used a crossbow to sever the rope, freeing her and delivering a fatal blow to the creature.

### The Final Blow

Shuwannu, drawing on the rage of a husband whose wife was murdered, unleashed his full power. The ground cracked beneath him as he overwhelmed Shamanu, stripping him of his name and rendering him powerless.

"I was a Guardian before I was a husband," Shuwannu said, his voice steady. "My duty comes first."

Shamanu, broken and defeated, surrendered.

### The Aftermath

The battlefield was eerily silent in the aftermath of the colossal battle. The smoke from fires still lingered in the air, and the smell of scorched flesh, broken earth, and spilled blood was overwhelming. The massive bodies of fallen Gremors lay scattered across the field, their grotesque forms motionless, while the Roman soldiers stood amongst the wreckage, battered but victorious.

*Honoring the Fallen*

Maximus and Conan walked through the battlefield, their steps heavy with grief and exhaustion. The bodies of fallen comrades littered the ground—brave men who had given their lives to hold the line. Among them were Lugo, Han, Lee, Ronan, and the priest, their lifeless forms a stark reminder of the cost of victory.

Maximus stopped before Lugo's body, kneeling to gently close his friend's eyes. "You were more than a warrior, Lugo. You were a brother," he said softly. Conan stood nearby, his sword planted in the ground, his head bowed in silent respect.

Together, they gathered the bodies of their fallen companions and oversaw their cremation in a grand pyre built at the edge of the battlefield. The flames roared high into the night sky, a tribute to the heroes who had fought so valiantly. Maximus spoke as the flames danced.

"They were not just men of Rome. They were giants among us—heroes whose deeds will echo through eternity. We honor their sacrifice and carry their memory with us." A flash of his heroic act.

*Di Vinci's Sacrifice*

At the base of the mountain, Shuwannu helped carry the lifeless body of Senator Di Vinci back to the Roman lines.

His face was serene in death, his hands still clutching the crossbow he had used in the battle.

Di Vinci: "I've carried this into every battle. It has given me luck. It's yours now." He handed Sheba a medallion.

Sheba: "Keep it. You'll need it more than I will." she smiled as she hung her whip on her hip. "The day I die, is the day I'm meant to. I'll feel safe knowing that you are safe." She added.

The soldiers, weary but resolute, saluted the pyre, their voices raised in a somber chant to honor the fallen. As he was escorted into Rome, Sheba joined the procession, holding back her floodgates, and in her hand was Di Vinci's medallion.

Sheba's reaction to his sacrifice was raw and emotional, showing how deeply she valued their bond.

In Rome, Sheba stepped forward during Di Vinci's funeral procession to deliver a heartfelt tribute. She placed the medallion he gave her on his casket as a symbol of their friendship.

"He taught me that even the weakest blade can shine when it's held with purpose. He was a warrior. He was my friend. And Rome owes him everything."

Maximus met Shuwannu at the camp, his face pale but determined. "He was the strategist behind this victory. Rome owes him more than it can ever repay."

Shuwannu nodded, his voice low. "He fought with honor, just as he lived. His courage and vision saved many lives today."

Di Vinci's body was wrapped in fine cloth, his face

covered with a golden mask symbolizing honor and sacrifice. He was to be returned to Rome for a hero's burial. His children, who had waited anxiously for his return, would be given royal titles in recognition of his bravery.

*Sealing the Eggs*

The surviving soldiers worked tirelessly to move the remaining Gremor eggs into a hidden cave. The entrance was sealed with tons of debris, reinforced with molten metal from the wreckage of their catapults and crossbows.

Maximus oversaw the operation, his voice carrying across the field. "These eggs are a reminder of what we faced today. Let them remain buried, a testament to what humanity can overcome when united."

The soldiers, though weary, worked with renewed purpose, knowing the weight of their actions would ensure the safety of future generations.

*Shuwannu's Departure*

Shuwannu stood atop a ridge overlooking the battlefield, his glowing armor dimmed but still radiant. The light of dawn broke over the horizon, illuminating the destruction below.

Maximus and Conan approached him, their steps hesitant.

"What happens now?" Maximus asked, his voice tinged with exhaustion.

Shuwannu turned to them, his expression unreadable. "I

take Shamanu back to my realm. He will face the council for his crimes against Earth and Alganu. His punishment will be decided there."

"And what about us?" Conan asked, his voice carrying a hint of bitterness. "We lost too many today. What do we tell the families of those who didn't return?"

Shuwannu's gaze softened. "Tell them the truth. That their loved ones saved an entire world. Their sacrifices will not be forgotten, not by me, nor by the people of Rome. You have my gratitude."

Maximus frowned. "And what about you, Shuwannu? Will we ever see you again?"

Shuwannu hesitated. "Guardians are bound by their duty, Maximus. But if Earth ever faces a threat like this again, I will come."

With that, Shuwannu turned and lifted the bound Shamanu into the air. The Red Guardian, now weak and powerless, hung limply as Shuwannu opened a shimmering portal. Before stepping through, he looked back one last time. "Thank you, my friends. For everything."

As the portal closed, Maximus and Conan stood in silence, the weight of the moment settling over them.


*Return to Rome*

Weeks later, the surviving soldiers marched into Rome to a hero's welcome. Crowds lined the streets, their cheers deafening as the tattered banners of the Legion waved proudly in the wind.

Maximus led the procession, his head held high despite

the losses weighing on him. Behind him were the bodies of their fallen, including Senator Di Vinci, carried on a gilded chariot draped in the banners of Rome.

Senator Aralus's absence was noted, and whispers spread through the crowd. Some called him a fool for leading an ill-fated charge; others labeled him a coward who sought glory and paid the price.

In the Senate chambers, Caesar addressed the assembly. "Today, Rome honors its heroes. General Maximus and his men faced the unimaginable and emerged victorious. Senator Di Vinci gave his life for our future, and his legacy will endure for generations."

The Senate erupted in applause, their previous rivalries forgotten in the face of shared triumph. Maximus stood silently, his mind far from the grandeur of the moment.

*A New Purpose*

That night, Maximus stood alone on the balcony of his quarters, gazing out over the city. The weight of the battle still pressed heavily on him. Conan joined him, a flask of wine in his hand.

"You look like you've aged a decade," Conan said, offering the flask.

Maximus chuckled faintly, taking a sip. "Feels like it, too."

"So, what's next for the great General Maximus?" Conan asked.

Maximus turned to him, his expression thoughtful. "We

rebuild. We make sure this never happens again. And we honor the sacrifices of those we lost."

Conan nodded, his gaze distant. "To the fallen, then. May their stories never fade."

Maximus raised the flask. "To the fallen."

As they drank, the city of Rome stretched out before them—a city saved by their courage and sacrifice. But both men knew that the peace they had won was fragile, and the future held its own challenges.

For now, though, they allowed themselves a moment of quiet reflection, knowing that the battle was over.

10

# EPILOGUE

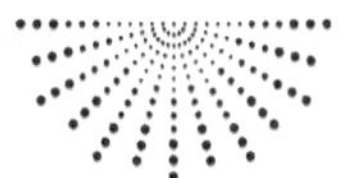

*The Trial of Shamanu*

The air shimmered with an ethereal light as Shuwannu stepped through the portal, Shamanu's limp form floating behind him. They emerged into the Great Hall of Guardians, a vast chamber of shimmering crystal and endless arches that stretched beyond sight. The walls pulsed faintly with a living energy, their hues shifting between soft blues and whites, reflecting the solemnity of the moment.

Seven seats formed a semi-circle at the far end of the hall, each occupied by a Guardian cloaked in the radiant colors of their station—green, black, yellow, brown, white, and violet. At the center sat the White Guardian, leader of the council, her presence both serene and commanding. Her eyes glowed with piercing intensity as she rose to address Shuwannu.

"Shuwannu, Blue Guardian of Alganu, you return to us

victorious yet burdened," she said, her voice resonating through the chamber. "What have you brought before this council?"

Shuwannu stepped forward, his face calm but stern. "I bring Shamanu, the Red Guardian, charged with betrayal, murder, and the unprovoked assault upon the Earth realm. He has used his power to sow chaos and death, violating the sacred laws that bind us as Guardians."

The other Guardians murmured among themselves, their voices low and filled with tension. Shamanu, now conscious but weakened, was lowered to his knees before the council. His crimson armor, once a symbol of his strength, was now dull and cracked, and his once-defiant eyes were clouded with exhaustion.

"Shamanu," the White Guardian said, her tone sharp, "you stand accused of crimes that threaten the balance of all realms. Do you deny these charges?"

Shamanu raised his head slowly, a faint smirk curling his lips. "Deny? No. I revel in them. The Earth realm was weak, unworthy of its protection. I sought to cleanse it and reshape it into something greater."

The Guardians erupted in outrage, their voices overlapping in a cacophony of condemnation. The White Guardian raised her hand, silencing them instantly.

"Your arrogance knows no bounds," she said, her voice icy. "Do you understand the magnitude of what you've done? You jeopardized not only the Earth realm but the very balance of the cosmos."

. . .

*The Sentence*

Shuwannu stepped forward, his voice calm but resolute. "I request that Shamanu be stripped of his powers and exiled to the Lost Grounds of Laladaru, where he can do no further harm."

The council deliberated, their voices a low hum as they debated the severity of the punishment. Finally, the White Guardian spoke. "Shamanu, by the will of this council, you are hereby stripped of your name, your powers, and your status as a Guardian. You will be exiled to the Lost Grounds of Laladaru, where you will spend eternity in isolation."

Shamanu laughed, a harsh, hollow sound. "Eternity in isolation? Do you truly believe that will stop me? You Guardians are blind to the truth. There are forces far greater than your council, and they are watching. You've only delayed the inevitable."

The Guardians exchanged uneasy glances, his words sowing a seed of doubt.

*The Twist*

As the White Guardian raised her hand to deliver the final decree, a sudden ripple of energy coursed through the hall. The crystal walls dimmed, and a low hum filled the air. The Guardians froze, their eyes scanning the chamber for the source of the disturbance.

A figure materialized in the center of the hall, cloaked in shadows. Its form was indistinct, shifting like smoke caught in a faint breeze. Its voice was deep and resonant, carrying an unsettling calm.

"You think this ends with Shamanu?" the figure said, addressing the council. "You are fools to believe that the balance remains intact. The Earth realm was but the first step. There are others, and the storm is coming."

The Guardians rose from their seats, their energies flaring as they prepared to confront the intruder. The White Guardian stepped forward, her voice commanding. "Who are you to intrude upon this sacred hall?"

The figure chuckled, the sound echoing ominously. "I am no one, and yet I am everything. You will know me soon enough. This is merely the beginning."

Before anyone could react, the figure vanished, leaving the hall in stunned silence.

*Shamanu's Parting Words*

As the Guardians exchanged uneasy glances, Shamanu laughed once more, his voice filled with mockery. "You see? You Guardians are relics, clinging to an order that no longer exists. You focus so much on me that you fail to see the larger picture. I may be exiled, but the forces at work will make your balance crumble."

Shuwannu stepped forward, his eyes blazing with determination. "You will answer for your crimes, Shamanu. Whatever storms come, the Guardians will stand against them."

Shamanu's smirk remained as he was lifted into the air by a surge of energy. A portal to the Lost Grounds of

Laladaru opened behind him, its swirling darkness a stark contrast to the radiant light of the hall.

As he was cast into the portal, Shamanu's voice echoed a chilling warning: "You can't stop what's coming, Shuwannu. You've only delayed the inevitable."


*The Council's Unease*

The portal closed, and silence filled the hall once more. The Guardians returned to their seats, their expressions grim. The White Guardian turned to Shuwannu. "You have done well, Shuwannu. But this disturbance concerns me. We must prepare for whatever lies ahead."

Shuwannu nodded. "I will return to the Earth realm. If it is the first target, then it must be protected."

The White Guardian hesitated before responding. "You have earned a reprieve, Shuwannu. But if you choose to return, know that the burden will be great."

The White Guardian addressed Shuwannu after Shamanu's exile, "Our power is drawn from the balance of realms. When one is thrown into chaos, the others are strained. Shamanu's actions disrupted that balance, and the Earth nearly fell."

"Then Earth must be protected. I will remain as its Guardian. I have made my choice," Shuwannu said.


*A New Threat*

As Shuwannu stepped through the portal back to the Earth realm, a dark presence lingered in the shadows of the Guardian's hall. Unseen by all, it whispered softly to itself.

"The Guardians are fractured. The Earth is vulnerable. And soon, all realms will fall."

Far away, in the sealed cave where the Gremor eggs lay buried, faint cracks began to form in the debris. A low, guttural hum emanated from within, growing stronger with each passing moment.

The storm was indeed coming.

*To Be Continued...*

# COMPREHENSIVE CHARACTER DESCRIPTION LIST

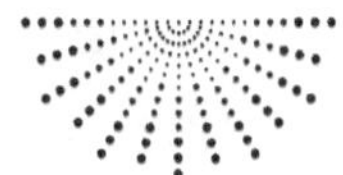

## MAJOR CHARACTERS

**1. Shuwannu (The Blue Guardian)**

Personality: Calm, wise, and dutiful. Struggles with personal loss but remains focused on maintaining cosmic balance. Loyal to his role as a Guardian.

Physical Features:

Height: 6"2 feet.

Lean, athletic build.

Radiant blue armor emitting a faint glow.

Piercing blue eyes that radiate wisdom and authority.

Origin: Guardian of Alganu, charged with balancing all realms. Lost his name and full powers after pursuing Shamanu to Earth.

Strength Rating: 10/10

Near-limitless strength, energy manipulation, and unmatched combat skills.

Skills:

Dual-wielding expert swordsman.

Telekinesis and energy field manipulation.

Exceptional strategist.

## 2. Shamanu (The Red Guardian)

Personality: Vengeful, ambitious, and cunning. Consumed by jealousy and hatred for Shuwannu. Charismatic yet manipulative.

Physical Features:

Height: 6'2".

Muscular build, jagged crimson armor.

Fiery red eyes full of anger and hatred.

Scars marking his descent into chaos.

Origin: Former Guardian of Alganu, now rogue. Fled to Earth after betraying the council.

Strength Rating: 9.5/10

Equal in power to Shuwannu but emotionally unstable.

Skills:

Brute-force combat.

Dark energy manipulation.

Skilled in psychological warfare.

## 3. General Maximus

Personality: Brave, determined, and fiercely loyal to Rome and his men. Balances duty with personal emotions.

Physical Features:

Height: 6 feet.

Muscular with broad shoulders and battle scars.

Deep-set eyes reflecting experience.

Origin: Born to a military family in Rome. Rose to prominence due to exceptional strategy and bravery.

Strength Rating: 8/10

Lacks supernatural powers but excels in leadership and physical combat.

Skills:

Master swordsman and tactician.

Skilled in inspiring and rallying troops.


## 4. Conan (Barbarian King)

Personality: Fierce, headstrong, and honorable. Thrives in battle and values loyalty and camaraderie.

Physical Features:

Height: 6'5".

Towering, heavily muscled, with braided hair and a thick beard.

Wears armor made from animal hides and scavenged metal.

Origin: Barbarian tribe leader who rose to power through sheer strength and strategic alliances.

Strength Rating: 7.5/10

Raw physical strength unmatched among humans.

Skills:

Proficient with heavy weapons like axes and hammers.

Skilled survivalist and tracker.

## 5. Senator Di Vinci

Personality: Ambitious, prideful, and driven by a desire for legacy. Seeks glory on the battlefield and in politics.

Physical Features:

Height: 5'10".

Lean with a polished appearance and sharp features.

Wears fine Roman armor.

Origin: A noble Roman senator with a long family history of governance.

Strength Rating: 6/10

Decent fighter but relies heavily on strategy and subordinates.

Skills:

Skilled orator and manipulator.

Proficient in defensive combat.

## 6. Lugo (The Russian Giant)

Personality: Quiet, stoic, and fiercely loyal. Protective of his comrades and unshakable in battle.

Physical Features:

Height: 7 feet.

Towering and heavily muscled, with pale skin and long blond hair.

Rugged, battle-worn appearance.

Origin: From the snowy wilderness of Russia. Became a mercenary after his village was destroyed.

Strength Rating: 7.5/10

Unmatched physical strength but slower due to his size.

Skills:

Expert with heavy weapons like hammers and axes.

Proficient in wrestling and survival techniques.

## 7. Han and Lee (The Asian Twins)

Personality: Loyal, resourceful, and mischievous. Known for their unbreakable bond and coordinated fighting style.

Physical Features:

Height: 5'9".

Han: Stocky, with short black hair.

Lee: Slim, with long tied-back black hair.

Wear lightweight armor suited for speed and agility.

Origin: From an Asian village, trained in martial arts from a young age.

Strength Rating: 6/10

Agile and precise but lack raw strength.

Skills:

Masters of dual-wielding daggers and short swords.

Proficient in acrobatics and stealth.

## 8. The Priest

Personality: Wise, calm, and spiritual. Acts as a moral compass for the group.

Physical Features:

Height: 5'8".

Slim build with serene features.

Wears simple robes and carries a small crossbow.

Origin: A scholar turned soldier to defend his beliefs.

Strength Rating: 5/10

Physically weaker but mentally strong.

Skills:

Proficient with ranged weapons.

Knowledgeable in herbs and medicine.

## 9. Sheba (The Huntress)

Personality: Fierce, independent, and highly intelligent. Sheba is a warrior with an unbreakable spirit, driven by survival instincts and an unyielding sense of justice. She commands respect with her confidence and tactical mind. Though hardened by battle, she carries a deep sense of loyalty to those she trusts.

Physical Features:

Height: 6'3"

Athletic, curvy build —powerful yet graceful in movement.

Thick, flowing black hair, often braided for battle.

Light-skinned Black woman, striking in appearance with sharp, captivating features.

Piercing dark eyes that reflect wisdom and intensity.

Wears practical yet elegant battle gear, designed for both agility and protection.

Origin:

Born into a warrior clan, Sheba was trained from childhood in the ways of survival, hunting, and combat. A master of the wild, she has fought and survived against both men and beasts, earning a reputation as a deadly hunter.

Strength Rating: 8.5/10

Exceptionally strong and agile, with heightened reflexes.

Skilled in both ranged and close-quarters combat.

Skills:

Master hunter and tracker, able to read the land and antici-pate danger.

Expert whip wielder— her thick razor-edged whip can

ensnare, disarm, and slice through foes with lethal precision.

Proficient swordswoman and dagger fighter, striking with speed and deadly accuracy.

Survivalist — capable of thriving in the harshest environments, adapting quickly to any challenge.


BEASTS


**1. Kiballangu (Gremors)**

Description:

Height: 10-12 feet tall.

Black, tar-like skin with scales harder than steel.

Massive claws and fangs dripping with slime.

Roar resembles a lion's, instilling fear.

Strengths:

Near-impenetrable hide and exceptional hearing.

Weaknesses:

Poor eyesight and vulnerable to precise strikes.


**2. The Breeder (Female Kiballangu)**

Description:

Height: 60 feet tall.

Massive, grotesque body covered in scales.

Emits a hum that summons offspring.

Strengths:

Extreme durability and rapid egg production.

Weaknesses:

Vulnerable during egg-laying.

**3. The Male (Kiballangu Patriarch)**
Description:
Similar size to the female breeder but faster and sleeker.
Strengths:
Tactical leader of Kiballangu packs.
Weaknesses:
Reckless when protecting the eggs.

ADDITIONAL CHARACTERS

**1. Senator Aralus**
Personality: Opportunistic and ambitious, always seeking personal glory.
Physical Features:
Slim with calculating eyes, always impeccably dressed.
Skills:
Skilled manipulator and negotiator.

**2. Senator Lucius**
Personality: Conservative and protective of Roman traditions.
Physical Features:
Stout and weathered, with gray hair and a commanding presence.
Skills:
Skilled debater and tactician.

### 3. Cesar Claudius

Personality: Politically astute and calculating, focused on maintaining Roman stability.

Physical Features:

Lean but strong, with gray hair and a polished appearance.

Skills:

Master diplomat and strategist.

www.ingramcontent.com/pod-product-compliance
Lightning Source LLC
Chambersburg PA
CBHW031144130726
47988CB00006B/2532